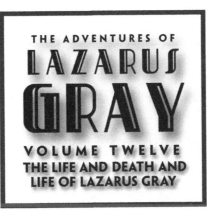

THE ADVENTURES OF
LAZARUS GRAY

VOLUME TWELVE
THE LIFE AND DEATH AND LIFE OF LAZARUS GRAY

BY **BARRY REESE**

Also available by Barry Reese from REESE UNLIMITED and published by Pro Se Press:

The Peregrine Omnibus - Volumes 1-3
The Adventures of Lazarus Gray
The Adventures of Gravedigger

Other Works
The Family Grace: An Extraordinary History
Rabbit Heart
The Damned Thing
The Second Book of Babylon
Assistance Unlimited: The Silver Age – Broken Empire
Worlds Apart

THE ADVENTURES OF LAZARUS GRAY, VOLUME TWELVE

A Reese Unlimited Book
Published by Pro Se Press

Cover By Jeffrey Hayes
Print Production and Book Design by Sean E. Ali
E-Book Design by Antonio lo Iacono and Marzia Marina

New Pulp Seal created by Cari Reese

Edited by Mike Hintze
Editor in Chief, Pro Se Productions-Tommy Hancock
Publisher and Pro Se Productions, LLC-Chief Executive Officer-Fuller Bumpers

Pro Se Productions, LLC
133 1/2 Broad Street
Batesville, AR, 72501
870-834-4022

editorinchief@prose-press.com
www.prose-press.com

THE ADVENTURES OF
LAZARUS
GRAY

VOLUME TWELVE
THE LIFE AND DEATH AND
LIFE OF LAZARUS GRAY

THE ADVENTURES OF
LAZARUS GRAY
VOLUME TWELVE
THE LIFE AND DEATH AND
LIFE OF LAZARUS GRAY

TABLE OF CONTENTS

THE SOVEREIGN
CITY PROJECT ™

SECRETS OF THE DEAD
THE ORIGIN OF LAZARUS GRAY

LAZARUS GRAY

IN SECRETS OF THE DEAD

BY BARRY REESE & GEORGE SELLAS

ASSISTANCE UNLIMITED
6196 ROBESON AVENUE

BORN TO WEALTHY SAN FRANCISCO PARENTS, RICHARD WINTHROP ATTENDED YALE UNIVERSITY AND GRADUATED WITH HONORS.

BUT ON THE DAY OF HIS GRADUATION, HE WAS APPROACHED BY WALTHER LUNT, WHO OFFERED HIM A PLACE WITHIN THE SHADOWY ORGANIZATION KNOWN AS **THE ILLUMINATI.**

HIS NATURAL INTEREST IN THE SUPERNATURAL SUDDENLY UNLEASHED, RICHARD ACCOMPANIED LUNT AROUND THE WORLD, INVESTIGATING THE UNKNOWN.

ALONG THE WAY, HE MET MIYA SHIMADA, A LOVELY JAPANESE-AMERICAN WHO WON HIS HEART.

BUT EVENTUALLY WINTHROP LEARNED THE TRUTH ABOUT THE ILLUMINATI AND THE VILE SECRETS THAT THEY POSSESSED. REBELLING, HE BECAME AN ENEMY TO THE MEN AND WOMEN HE HAD ONCE TRUSTED.

SHOT AND LEFT FOR DEAD ON THE SHORES OF SOVEREIGN CITY, RICHARD WINTHROP HAD NO MEMORY OF WHO OR WHAT HE WAS. THE ONLY CLUE TO HIS IDENTITY WAS A SMALL MEDALLION WITH THE WORDS 'LAZARUS GRAY' STAMPED UPON IT.

UNAWARE THAT LAZARUS GRAY HAD BEEN THE FALSE IDENTITY OF THE ILLUMINATI'S FOUNDER, WINTHROP TOOK THE NAME AS HIS OWN, IN THE HOPES THAT IT WOULD DRAW OUT THOSE WHO KNEW THE TRUTH ABOUT HIS PAST.

RESURRECTED AS A HERO, LAZARUS GRAY NOW FIGHTS TO MAKE UP FOR THE EVIL ACTS HE TOOK PART IN WITH THE ILLUMINATI. AIDED BY OTHERS WHO HAVE SIMILAR PASTS, LAZARUS GRAY HELPS MAKE SURE THAT THE INNOCENTS OF SOVEREIGN CITY CAN SLEEP PEACEFULLY IN THEIR BEDS!

THE LIFE AND DEATH AND
LIFE OF LAZARUS GRAY

AN ADVENTURE STARRING LAZARUS GRAY

Recently...

MORGAN SLIPPED OUT of his room just past midnight, having waited until all of 6196 Robeson Avenue was silent. He wore blue silk pajamas embroidered with his initials on the pocket and slippers - all the better to ensure that he made as little noise as possible as he stole into his friend's private study. He made sure to close the door as gently as possible and didn't bother turning on the desk lamp until he was sure that no one had heard him enter.

The room was lined with bookshelves containing tomes on every topic imaginable. Morgan had been in the room so many times that he'd long ago stopped paying attention to the details... but now he peered intently at every shelf, looking for something that might indicate a hidden door. He hoped to find nothing... but he knew that he would. That was his sister he had talked to beneath the Grendel Tree and she had told him this.

He spotted it on his second look-through of the shelves: an oversized copy of the Bible bound in leather, jutting just a bit farther off the shelf than it should have. Reaching out with a trembling hand, Morgan gave the book a pull... and the entire wall suddenly swung inward, revealing a darkened room beyond. He could see nothing of what lay inside but he heard the sounds of bubbling water, making him think of aquarium fish tanks.

He pushed on into the gloom, the false wall swinging shut behind him. Reaching out with his hands, he felt along the walls until he found a light switch. When he activated it, his heart seemed to jump up from his chest into his throat... he'd thought many times about what he might find in this room but never in his wildest imaginings had he envisioned anything like this.

The room was roughly equal in size to the team's briefing room, with a metallic table in the center and several rolling chairs situated around it. Atop the table were a number of books, writing instruments and a small tray containing the silver bullets that had caused so much trouble as of late.

It was the things that lined the room that were most shocking. There were eight tubes, connected by a variety of tubes and pipes to the wall. Within each tube was a bubbling fluid that wasn't quite water, being a bit too thick for that, and within the fluid were bodies, one in each tube. They were all naked, eyes tightly closed as if in slumber, and breathing masks covered their noses and mouths. The one closest to him was shockingly familiar and Morgan moved to stand open-mouthed in front of it, his eyes moving up and down the female form within.

Shaking his head as if to clear it, he moved on to the next... and then to the next... his confusion and horror mounting with each recognizable face that he gazed upon.

It made no sense but the fact that Lazarus had hidden all of this, like some mad scientist, made him certain that the truth had to be something sinister.

It was when he looked in the last tank that his heart truly broke. He saw his own face mirrored back at him, identical to the one he saw every morning when he shaved... but sans the most recent scars and bruises that he'd picked up while in Africa.

Glancing back at the other tubes, he saw the others, all looking pristine and new... Samantha, Abby, Eun, Kelly, even Lazarus himself. For a moment Morgan why there wasn't a duplicate of Bob floating in one of the tanks but then he reasoned that perhaps the man's plant/human hybrid nature played a part.

The door to the room swung open and Morgan whirled about in alarm. His hand dropped to the pocket of his pajamas, where his pistol hung heavily. He paused when he saw it was Lazarus - even with all the questions racing through his mind, he wasn't prepared to draw a weapon on his friend.

Not yet.

Lazarus didn't seem surprised to find Morgan. Instead, he merely looked tired, as if he was preparing himself for an argument he'd had too many times before. "Good evening, Morgan," he said, closing the door behind him. "There's a sensor located next to the door," he said, gesturing towards a small penny-sized device located on the wall near the ceiling. "It lets me know if someone comes in here."

Without preamble, Morgan asked, "What the hell is all this...?"

Walking over to the metal table, Lazarus picked up a few loose papers and began organizing them into a small stack. Are you aware that we share casefiles with some others in the city? Doc Daye, Gravedigger's crew..." Morgan shook his head and Lazarus continued. "A few years ago Gravedigger uncovered something strange going on at Drake Island. I won't bore you with all the details but someone was making copies of people - he called them clones but they were also called 'ghosts' by some. Using a series of brilliant techniques, this man was able to grow new bodies of people from whom he had taken certain skin and blood samples. Their personalities and memories were held intact, stored in their DNA. The one drawback was that each of these entities only had the memories up to the time of their cloning - they wouldn't be aware of anything that had occurred after that first sample was taken. In order to get around that, you would need to have samples taken on a regular basis so that if the original died, you'd have a new clone emerge that would have memories as close to the time of death as possible. Knowledge of their clone status was shown to have a detrimental effect on the patients so it was advisable to keep that from them and let them believe they were the original."

Morgan stared at him for a moment, letting it all sink in. "Doctor Hancock's physicals... he's always taking blood samples."

Lazarus looked at him. "Yes."

"Because you want to have copies of us around in case we die."

"Not just you - me, too. It's a safeguard for all of us."

"And if I croaked, you'd just dump this... copy of me... out of the tank and nobody would be the wiser?" Morgan shook his head. "That's just sick. You know it wouldn't work, right? That thing couldn't pass for me. Somebody would figure it out."

Lazarus said nothing, merely staring at him with a grave expression.

Morgan's shoulders began to slump and he asked, "You've already done it, haven't you? Who died...?"

"All of you, at one time or another."

"No," Morgan whispered, turning away from his friend. The implications were staggering and he knew he had to tell the others, let them know. Even if Lazarus had the best of intentions, this was too much... he should have told them, asked them if they wanted this. Even his own wife...!

"I know how you're feeling, Morgan... but after I came back from Hell, I knew that I had to take precautions. We all rely on each other and losing even one member of our family would be too much."

"You're not God, Lazarus," Morgan replied, rubbing his chin. He looked towards the door, planning to move towards it. "And if you think I'm going to stay silent on this, you're even crazier than I thought."

"It's not the first time."

Morgan turned quickly. "What do you mean?"

"It's not the first time you've figured it out... it's not always you, though. Last time it was Samantha. About six months ago."

Morgan's heart skipped a beat. "Please tell you didn't--"

"I protected all of you. I protected us. I know it seems awful, Morgan, but you have to trust me."

"Or what? You'll kill me and replace me with another version of me?" Morgan shoved his hand into his pocket and seized hold of his pistol. What happened next was as fast as it was brutal - Lazarus spun about, launching a kick that caught Morgan on the side of his chin and snapped his neck in one clean hit.

Lazarus stood there for a moment after it was done, feeling a mixture of shame and relief. His lies would remain unknown and he felt certain that, at the core of it all, he was doing the right thing. When he had 'died', the rest of the team had taken dangerous risks to bring him back… and earlier today Abby had voiced the secret truth that bound them all together: what would they do without each other? Lazarus knew what would happen… their carefully crafted world would fall apart and they'd all drift back to the way they'd been before they'd come together.

He knelt besides Morgan's corpse and touched it gently. "Sleep well, Morgan. You'll be back soon."

PROLOGUE

May 1892

A SMALL CONVOY of horse-drawn carriages emerged from the trees into a clearing near a farmhouse located on the outskirts of Sovereign City. The carriages drove on past a lake, their wheels throwing up mud and muck as they approached the home, which was in the middle of two landmarks - a grain silo on the left and a barn on the right. When the lead carriage decided they had come close enough, its driver raised a hand to signal the others to come to a halt. People jumped down and began to unload boxes, all of which were carried and dropped just outside the barn. Some of the boxes were so heavy that three or four men strained to lift them.

A man in uniform - gray jacket and jodhpurs - also leaped from one of the carriages. He adjusted his hat and looked around with obvious disgust at the location. A gun was holstered at his hip and he put one hand atop the handle as he slowly moved towards the barn. Felled trees lay beside the shimmering lake and the air smelled of spring and sawdust. It was already warm and there was no shade to be seen as all the trees had been cut down.

"Mr. McQuarry?" one of the men yelled and the man in the hat turned to look at him.

"Yes?"

"The boxes are unloaded. What should we do now?"

Gerald McQuarry rubbed the stubble on his chin and paused. A part of him wanted to forget this whole business - it wasn't too late for him to tell his men to load everything back up on the carts and take him back to town. From there he could either continue as things had been or he could start selling things off piecemeal to pay for a new start in another city, maybe someplace far out west.

He knew that wasn't going to be possible, though. Once you received a message from L'Homme Fantastique, there was nothing to do but play the game... or die.

The latter was what had happened to Little Tony. The Italian mobster had refused to recognize what was happening. He'd continued leading his gang, not doing the first thing to dismantle his empire. He thought himself untouchable but L'Homme Fantastique had proved him wrong. The Frenchman had somehow snuck past two dozen armed guards stationed around the boundaries of Tony's property... and slit the man's throat as he lay in bed next to his newest wife, who had slept through the entire thing.

McQuarry had decided to play along, at least for now. The mysterious Frenchman had left clear instructions: Gerald was to gather up every knife, every gun, and every piece of ammunition that his boys possessed - he was to then box them up and bring them here, to an address included along with the note. McQuarry would then meet with L'Homme Fantastique and the two men would engage in a game of chance... if Gerald won, he'd be free to leave with his life, as long as he swore to turn over a new leaf. However, if he lost, McQuarry's life would be forfeit.

On the surface, it sounded insane - but those were the rules by which L'Homme Fantastique had carved out a reputation for himself. No one knew where he had come from, though his French accent made it clear that his origins lay in Europe. How old he was... what he truly looked like, free of shadows and a low-brimmed hat... why he conducted himself by such a strange code of honor... all of these were mysteries to be savored by the town's gossips and reporters.

"Sir...?"

McQuarry realized that his man was still waiting for a response. He reached into the pocket of his coat and withdrew a small billfold.

He withdrew a wad of money, pressing it into the fellow's hand. "Take everyone back into town - and buy your wife a nice dress."

"You're staying here, sir?" the man asked, looking down at the money with wide eyes.

"I am. Now go and get out of here!" McQuarry said gruffly. Within minutes, the caravan was back on its way, leaving their erstwhile leader to stand outside the barn door. He took out a cigarette, lit it with a match, and enjoyed the smoke before he finally ground out the butt beneath the heel of his shoe and turned back to the door. Without knocking, he gave the handle a yank and it opened easily, revealing a darkened interior with a straw floor. The barn was lit by a single candle that rested atop a circular table at which there were two chairs. One of them was empty, its back to the door... the other was occupied by a man dressed in a flamboyant purple suit and tie. A hat was perched on his head, tilted forward to obscure its wearer with a broad brim. A feather, dyed the same monochromatic shade as its owner's suit, was fitted inside the hatband. This was L'Homme Fantastique and despite his somewhat foppish appearance, he froze the blood in McQuarry's veins

"Welcome, mon amie," L'Homme Fantastique said with a thick French accent. There was a deck of playing cards set in front of him and Fantastique lifted them in one before beginning to shuffle. "Come. Sit. I am so glad that you have decided to play the game. Life is boring without play, non?"

McQuarry sat down, straining to see the other man's features in the gloom. He thought he saw high cheekbones, cupid-bow lips and a bit of scarring on the right side of the face but with the flickering shadows, he was unsure how much of it was his imagination. "Can't you just let me go? Skip the whole game of chance routine? I've done what you asked."

"I appreciate all you've done, mon ami. I know it couldn't have been easy for you - it took a long time to craft an empire like yours and dismantling it was quite painful, I'm sure." The mysterious man in purple leaned forward and added, "The game, though, is tradition... and I am a man bound by what has come before. So let us play." With skilled hands, Fantastique began dealing cards, make sure that both men had the same number of cards - ten in all. "We shall play Knock Rummy[1]. You are familiar with the game?" he asked, placing the remaining cards in the center of the table and flipping the top one to expose a five of clubs.

McQuarry nodded slowly, the pounding of his heart seeming to rise up into his throat. There was no escaping the truth: his survival would depend on skill and luck... the whims of chance.

---

1 Knock Rummy is a game that goes back at least as far as 1905 so 1892 here isn't much of a stretch. It and a game known as Conquian were melded together and tweaked to create the better-known Gin Rummy.

CHAPTER I
WILDFIRE

Summer 1943

LAZARUS GRAY SPAT out a tooth, a dull throb growing in strength behind his eyes. He was having trouble breathing, a combination of the acrid smoke that burned his throat and lungs and the bruised - possibly broken - ribs that he'd sustained. He slowly rose to his feet, wiping his mouth with the back of a hand. A section of the roof collapsed behind him and the sudden bursts of flame momentarily left him in silhouette, outlining the figure of a man in the prime of life, with the short of rangy build that resembled that of Hollywood star Cary Grant.

Fires burned out of control around him as the ancient house known locally as the Fuller Estates hurried along towards the end of its long life. The house had been erected in 1804 and had long been noted for its architectural beauty. Situated on a hill overlooking downtown, it had been depicted on postcards and paintings almost from the day its building had been completed.

Facing Lazarus was a bald man dressed in a thick gray bodysuit and boots. He held the nozzle of an M2 flamethrower in his hands, the tubing linked up to the hourglass frame mounted on his back. Dubbed The Fire Bug, this man was actually Lorenzo Dekalb, a former fire fighter that had lost his job when he'd been accused of starting some of the very blazes that he'd helped snuff out.

The Fire Bug seemed completely unaware that Lazarus was upright.

His eyes were locked on the flames that were spreading by the second. His expression was one of sexual lust and Lazarus was certain that if the bodysuit hadn't been quite so thick, an erection would have been visible.

Suddenly looking at Lazarus, the arsonist asked in a hoarse voice, "Isn't it beautiful? The flames are like little bodies, dancing and writhing... I only wish I could touch them." He held up one gloved hand. "Underneath, I have so many scars... sometimes I just can't help myself."

"Your worst scars are *under* the skin, Lorenzo... but I can get you help. Put down the flamethrower and let's get out of here." Lazarus walked slowly towards his opponent, stretching out a hand. If he could close enough, maybe he could seize the Fire Bug's wrist...

Shaking his head, the Fire Bug replied, "No... I'm going to stay here. If I leave, I'm going to jail or to a hospital. No way I'm going to spend my days in a nuthouse. I'm going to let her hug me. I'm going to let her touch warm me from head to toe." He jerked the nozzle in the hero's direction when Lazarus took a step too close towards him. "I'll set you on fire. Go! Leave!"

"I can't do that."

"Why not? Nobody's here except you and me... just let me die." Lorenzo's face contorted in agony and he screeched out every word. "I'm sick! I know that! I want what I can't have... and it drives me crazy! Nobody will miss me!"

"You have an ex-wife and three children," Lazarus said, flinching as a section of the staircase leading to the second floor suddenly gave way, falling to the floor with a loud thud.

"Suzy won't let me see my kids!" Lorenzo turned the nozzle towards his own face and added, "You can die with me or you can get out of here. Either way, I'm a dead man. Let me go in peace!"

Lazarus saw The Fire Bug start to squeeze the firing trigger and he lunged forward, knocking the man down and sending the entire flamethrower careening to the floor. The arsonist fought like a wildman, a keening sound coming from his tightly compressed lips. He twisted in an attempt to crawl into the flames but Lazarus held him firmly until he could draw back a fist - he punched The Fire Bug in the face, shattering his nose. A second punch sent Lorenzo flying into a concussion-induced slumber.

Scrambling back to an upright position, Lazarus reached down and lifted the stocky man up onto his shoulders. A grunt escaped his lips as he rose to his full height, bearing the man's weight. He looked around for an exit from the burning building but everywhere he looked all he saw were walls of flame.

He'd pursued The Fire Bug to the Fuller Estates while the rest of his associates in Assistance Unlimited were occupied with cases of their own: The Black Terror and his junior partner, Tim, were rousting Fifth Columnists near the harbor; Samantha Grace and Eun Jiwon were providing bodyguard protection to a socialite whose ex-boyfriend had threatened her life; and Morgan Watts, Abigail Cross, and Kelly Gray were digging through a set of supposedly-cursed books written in Latin that had been unearthed when an old building in downtown had been demolished.

All of this meant that Lazarus was on his own - there was no cavalry waiting to swoop in and save him. He would have to find his own means of escape. Quickly calculating his chances of success, he decided that moving to his right was his best option - the fires there had spread over some flowery curtains but there was an open window beneath them - the oxygen coming in from outside had fed the flames but Lazarus still thought the opening was big enough that he'd be able to leap through head first... though that was without having a man on his shoulders.

Hurrying towards the window, Lazarus grunted as he maneuvered his foe's bulk and hefted the unconscious man through the opening. He threw him as far and as hard as he could, hoping that The Fire Bug would land outside the flames that had spread out onto the grass. Through the din of the crackling fire and the crashing of support beams, Lazarus thought he heard the clanging bells of a fire truck. Good, he mused, perhaps they'd be able to salvage something of this historic old home.

A sudden upswell of fire made Lazarus flinch and draw back. The window was a far less appealing exit now but Lazarus still thought it his best option. He took several steps back and then ran, lowering his shoulders and jumping through the wall of fire and the open window. He landed in a rolling fall, his body engulfed for a moment in heat, before coming out past The Fire Bug. He spun about, ignoring the way his shirt was smoking and the light burns that covered his arms and face. Seizing the villain under the shoulders, he pulled him to safety and quickly checked to make sure the man was breathing. Satisfied that the arsonist would survive long enough to face a judge, Lazarus sat down heavily in the grass, which is where he was when the fire engine came hurtling down the drive and skidded to a stop a safe distance from the inferno.

Lazarus greeted several of the firefighters by name, having grown familiar with them over the course of his career in Sovereign City. It hadn't always been his home, of course - he had come to the city ten years ago, having survived an assassination attempt on the part of the Illuminati, a shadowy organization bent on world domination. He'd lost his memory for a time after this, losing his true identity as Richard Winthrop... he'd been reborn as Lazarus Gray, adopting a new home, a new family and a new mission.

He had never regretted the events that had led him here - this town and its people were his and he would do whatever it took to protect them.

Even if that meant killing them.

—❦—

San Francisco

JACK KNAPP STOOD motionless at the entrance to the abandoned warehouse. The floor was covered with a fine covering of dust - but even though the only illumination came from moonlight, Knapp could see that someone had recently walked through this area. Footprints could clearly be seen in the dust and he knew that he was on the right track - the man he had been following for the past hour had indeed ducked into this location to try and lose him.

Jack was a well-chiseled man with ebony black hair and a more-than-passing resemblance to actor Gary Cooper. He was dressed in a light blue tunic with a white collar-stripe and pants of a darker hue - he liked to think of the outfit as his "working clothes," as he wore them when he was putting plain old Jack to sleep for a bit... and giving free reign to the mystery man dubbed Blue Fire by the press.

Jack Richard Knapp had always loved science and he had thrown himself into his studies, earning high praise from his professors en route to a PhD. His research had brought him to the attention of the Nazis, who had attempted to sabotage one of his experiments. Caught up in the resulting explosion, Jack should have by all rights been killed... but some higher power had seemed to think he still had a part to play in the world. Jack not only survived but he found he was gifted with certain incredible abilities: he was able to cover himself with a fiery blue aura that didn't generate heat but which allowed him to fly and become intangible. Initially, his powers had faded after only a couple hours' use but practice had increased this and he was rarely taxed by even a full days' use of his blue flame.

As Blue Fire, Jack had become a notable hero along America's West Coast - his clashes with German secret agents like Tanya Gerhst had become popular fodder for the newspapers. Of his many foes, however, one stood head and shoulders above the rest - the saboteur known only as Frost. With the aid of special pills developed by the finest scientists in the Third Reich, Frost gained the ability to project ice from his own body. Frost had used his power to freeze American ships in hopes of disrupting their ability to take needed goods to nations that were warring with Germany... but Blue Fire had disrupted his scheme, earning him the Nazi's wrath.

It was Frost that had led Blue Fire to this tattered old warehouse located on the San Francisco harbor. Originally the building had belonged to Hancock Shipping, an importer/exporter that had gone belly-up during the Great Depression. It had sat abandoned for over eight years and the number of bottles that littered the ground outside made it clear that it had become the squatting site for winos and other transients.

Blue Fire had learned that Frost was back in town, intent on disrupting a gathering of American scientists. In his secret identity, Blue Fire was in attendance and when the keynote speaker had been found frozen to death, he recognized his old enemy's handiwork. After doing some detective work, Blue Fire had managed to locate several people that had spotted a fellow matching Frost's description and eventually he'd located a cabbie that had picked up and dropped Frost off from the harbor.

Summoning the flaming aura that gave him his heroic name, Blue Fire moved into the gloomy interior of the warehouse. Huge crates were stacked throughout, most of them labeled FOR STORAGE on all sides. "If you're in here, Frost, you might as well surrender. I know you murdered Prof. Forrester."

"Herr Forrester chose to die - I offered him the chance to come to Germany and put his skills to the use of the Reich." Frost's voice echoed in the warehouse, seeming to come from all directions at once. Blue Fire looked around, trying to catch a glimpse of him but he failed to do so.

With a grim smile, Blue Fire allowed himself to become intangible - he passed right through a wall of crates to his left, hoping that he would catch his enemy by surprise. The gambit worked, as he spotted Frost waiting at what would have been the perfect spot for an ambush - the German stood at the next bend of the makeshift maze, his hands generating a fine spray of mist as he stood on edge, expecting Blue Fire to walk right into his line of attack.

Clenched his hands into fists, Blue Fire solidified his physical form and charged at Frost. The Nazi turned just in time to see a right hand coming right towards his face. The blow shattered the villain's nose, sending a spray of blood into the air.

To his credit, Frost did not fold at this point. Even as he was tumbling back, his hands went up and freezing cold exploded out from his palms. Blue Fire felt the chill immediately and he fell back into intangibility just in time to avoid being turned into a block of living ice.

Frost roared at the hero, inadvertently spraying the air with droplets of blood. Blue Fire allowed these to pass through him, then became tangible once again as he delivered a roundhouse punch that sent Frost back into a wall of crates. These tumbled over, striking the floor with a loud crash, and spilling their contents all over the floor… and Blue Fire suddenly realized with alarm that this warehouse had not been abandoned for quite so long as he thought. Stuffed inside the boxes were explosive devices of German design - Frost wasn't here in San Francisco merely to interfere with a scientific conference. The man was planning something much bigger and much more horrific…

Plucking up one of the devices, Frost grinned maniacally, blood still dripping from his nose and running down over his lips and chin. "You might survive an explosion from all of these, Blue Fire - but there are plenty of innocent men and women that work here on the harbor. Are you willing to have their deaths on your conscience?"

"You wouldn't set those things off," Blue Fire said, his eyes narrowing. "You're many things but suicidal has never been one of them."

"There's a difference between merely killing oneself and becoming a martyr," Frost pointed out. "Your intangibility works fine on bullets but I'm not positive that your power would protect you against a warehouse full of explosives. Should we test it? All it would take is for me freeze this device. It's been set to detonate if its internal temperature drops past a certain point."

Blue Fire paused before answering. The upper limits of his powers had, indeed, not been fully tested. In truth, he did think he would survive an explosion, even one as massive as this one might be… but he was no in hurry to experiment with either his own life or those of the men and women that might in the surrounding areas.

Girding his loins, Blue Fire decided that in an instance like this, he would rather go out in a proverbial blaze of glory rather than wait for Frost to make the decision for him. He pushed off with his feet, launching himself through the air - in addition to allowing him the power of intangibility, the azure aura gave him the ability of flight.

Frost's eyes widened in surprise as Blue Fire hurtled past him, reaching down to snatch the explosive out of his hands. The German scrambled to seize another bomb but Blue Fire had already landed, set the explosive down as gently as time allowed, and kicked out with a foot. The heel of his boot caught Frost in the forehead and he hissed with pain, grabbing at his face.

As the villain rolled away, he tossed out shards of razor-sharp ice in Blue Fire's general direction. They passed harmlessly through the hero's body, however, and the Nazi muttered several curses in his native tongue as his vision cleared and he saw Blue Fire descending upon him.

"Nighty-night, Fritz," Blue Fire said as he delivered one final punch to the villain's face.

"Nice work," someone said, their voice carrying a note of authority.

Blue Fire whirled about, wondering if Frost had been working with another Nazi agent... but he stopped short when he saw a man that was arguably America's most famous hero.. "Holy heck," Blue Fire whispered under his breath. "You're The Fighting Yank!"

"You recognize me?" the Yank replied, a smile on his face and a twinkle in his eye. The man that stood before Blue Fire was instantly recognizable in his garb, which consisted of a domino mask, a tri-cornered hat, square buckles, white shirt emblazoned with an image of the American flag, blue pants and black shoes. A green cape with red lining completed the ensemble and while the getup might have looked silly on some, The Fighting Yank somehow carried it off with aplomb.

"Of course I do! You were one of the inspirations for me to become a member of the long johns brigade!" Blue Fire allowed his aura to fade and he stepped forward to offer a sturdy handshake. "Is it true that bullets bounce off you?"

"Small caliber only. Of course, you've got that beat, haven't you? You can just let the bullets pass right through you."

"I wish I could take credit for that one - I was caught up in an accident, that's all."

"That kind of thing happens more than you might think," the Yank said, reaching up to adjust his hat. "I hope you don't mind but I've already called in the authorities - they're waiting outside to take Frost and his bombs into custody."

Blue Fire blinked in surprise. "How long have you been watching?"

"A little while - I didn't want to interfere since I knew you two had a history. Figured it might be personal."

"He hates me more than I hate him," Blue Fire shrugged. "Were you working the same case? Tracking down Frost?"

"Actually I'm here for you. How about we go someplace a little more private and have a chat?"

— ∞ —

'PRIVATE' TURNED OUT to be the roof of a nearby building. The two heroes had climbed up a fire escape after ensuring that Frost and his explosives were safely in the care of the FBI.

Blue Fire ran a hand through his hair and smiled at the question the other man had asked him. "You're right - not wearing a mask puts me at risk of people uncovering my real identity… but the blue aura that I can summon not only makes my face blurry in photographs but it seems to have some sort of unnerving effect on people that see me in action. I've literally saved someone's life as the Blue Fire and then shook their hands as Jack Knapp a couple of hours later - and they don't recognize me at all!" Blue Fire laughed softly and said, "By the way, the name's Jack Knapp… though I suspect you already know that, don't you? The way those government guys were jumping at your every word, I think it's safe to say you're a G-man, right?"

"You're a bright guy… but I'm no G-Man. I have a lot of contacts with the government, though. Uncle Sam's been nice enough to deputize me in a few different capacities, Mr. Knapp."

Blue Fire waved a hand. "Call me Blue Fire… or Jack. Never call me Mr. Knapp - that's my dad."

The Fighting Yank placed a hand on Blue Fire's shoulder. "I need you, Jack… Your country needs you. Something very wrong is happening in Sovereign City… and I'll be honest with you: if it's half as bad as I think it is, I'm going to need your power."

"I heard you work sometimes with Assistance Unlimited - is that true?"

"You're a fan of theirs?"

Jack grinned sheepishly. "Well, I might have a little bit of a crush on Samantha Grace."

"I'll be sure to introduce you." The Yank's face grew serious. "Will you join me?"

"How could any red-blooded American say no? My only question is: how full-time a job is this? Do I need to call the University I work at and tell them I'm out for the duration of the war?"

The Fighting Yank released his hold on Jack's shoulder. His cape was blowing in the breeze and Jack couldn't help but notice that everything the famous hero did only reinforced the impression that he'd stepped right out of a Norman Rockwell painting. "No, no -- I have no idea how long it'll take but I can't imagine it'll be more than a few weeks at the most. Trust me, you won't lose your position at the University. A signed letter from FDR should be good enough to ensure they know you're working on something important, don't you think?"

Blue Fire grinned. "I think the Dean will be falling all over himself to make sure I'm given all the leave that I need. So when do we leave for Sovereign?"

"You have time to go home and pack some things - then you need to meet me at the airport at dawn."

"And we'll meet up with Lazarus Gray when we get to Sovereign?"

"I'm... not sure about that, son. You see, Lazarus Gray's the problem we might have to deal with."

CHAPTER II
THICKER THAN WATER

LAZARUS GRAY'S HEADQUARTERS was located at one of the most famous addresses in Sovereign City - indeed, it was known by a large number of people all across the country. This was because the group that Lazarus belonged to was famous for helping those in need, no matter their race, political affiliation or ability to pay.

The headquarters of Assistance Unlimited was part of a city block that was entirely owned by Lazarus. What had once been an unassuming neighborhood had been transformed into the beating heart of Gray's law-abiding enterprise.

The centerpiece of his holdings was a three-story structure that had once been a hotel. Gray's associates used the first floor, while the second had been gutted and converted into one large room that was used for meetings, briefings and research. The third floor was off-limits to everyone but Lazarus and his family, serving as their private residence. He lived there with his wife Kelly and their three-year-old son Ezekiel.

Facing the former hotel were several storefronts, all of which had closed down at the dawn of the Great Depression. They were now quite empty, though each was equipped with sensitive monitoring equipment that allowed Lazarus and his companions to keep track of every car or pedestrian that stepped foot onto Robeson Avenue.

Lazarus parked his car in the underground garage beneath his home, entering the building via the elevator. When he stepped out onto into the lobby, he was greeted by the familiar sounds and sights of his extended family: the others had returned from their various missions and the group's children - Samantha's daughter Emily and Lazarus' own son Ezekiel - were playing and laughing on the carpeted floor. There were several unexpected faces in the pack, as well -- Mayor Mortimer Quinn; Bob's girlfriend Jean and his young ward, Tim; Eun's lover, Eddie; the young redhead named Sally Weatherby, who in truth was no less than Thor's daughter Thrud; Samantha's half-sister Charity; and Doctor Hancock, Assistance Unlimited's long-time physician[2].

Kelly spotted her husband and moved away from the rest of the group. She gave him a hug and pulled back, whispering in his ear, "We found several books that were interesting. I've got them waiting for you in the study."

"Thank you," he replied. He held on to her hand as he greeted the others - when Zeke ran to him, he finally released Kelly and scooped his little boy up, nuzzling his son and giving him a loving squeeze.

"Happy birthday, daddy!" the toddler yelled and Lazarus looked over the boy's shoulder to see that the group had parted enough to reveal a cake adorned with ten lit candles.

Lazarus looked somewhat confused as he set his son down. "My birthday isn't until September... that's nearly three months from now."

Kelly shook her head and grinned, "That's Richard Winthrop's birthday, silly... but Lazarus Gray crawled from the sea exactly ten years ago tonight, washing up on the shores of Sovereign City Bay. Can't believe you forgot that."

"I'm not overly sentimental." Lazarus nodded at his friends, accepting their handshakes and hugs. With no relatives left from his Winthrop days, maybe Kelly was right -- the night he became Lazarus Gray was probably a more suitable day to celebrate.

Morgan cleared his throat and said, "Alright, everyone, I'll lead the singing." The team's eldest member looked dapper in his suit, his trademark pencil-thin mustache perfectly trimmed and waxed.

Lazarus looked at his friend and suddenly a wave of nausea came

---

2 A few of these deserve special mention - Charity Grace and Mortimer Quinn have both been known as Gravedigger in the past, while Sally/Thrud teamed up with Assistance Unlimited back in Volume 9 of this series.

over him. He saw Morgan, lying on the floor, his neck broken… and Lazarus himself stood over him, having killed him with a roundhouse kick. Lazarus swayed and might have sunk to his knees if Dr. Hancock hadn't grabbed him by the elbow.

"Laz! You okay?" Samantha asked, moving up beside Kelly and the doctor. "You look like you just saw a ghost!"

Blinking several times, Lazarus turned his gaze to the floor… wherever he looked, he saw dead people: Samantha with a bullethole between her eyes, Kelly floating facedown in a lake, Eun with a gaping wound in his neck.

Hancock eased Lazarus into a chair and warned everyone to stay back so that their friend and leader could have room to breathe. "What's happening?" Hancock asked, reaching to check his employer's pulse. "Difficulty breathing? Tightness in the chest?"

Lazarus shook his head and took several deep breaths. Gradually, his vision returned to normal… these people were his loved ones and they each wore expressions of concern - but they were unharmed. "I'm fine. I think I just inhaled too much smoke while fighting The Fire Bug."

"We should get you to my office," Hancock said. "I can run some tests--"

"No," Lazarus said emphatically. "I appreciate the concern but I'm all right."

Hancock looked hard at Lazarus, knowing that once the man had made up his mind, it was nearly impossible to change it. With a sigh of resignation, the physician stood up and spread his hands. "I've done all I can do, then. If you change your mind, you know I make house calls."

Kelly glanced at her husband and then turned to their friends. "Let's start cutting into the cake, shall we?" Her attempts to deflect everyone's attention proved successful and as Samantha began cutting pieces and placing them onto plates, Kelly moved closer to her husband. She let him take her hand and then she whispered without looking at him, "What's going on with you, Lazarus? That's the third time in the last two weeks I've seen you do that… whatever *that* is."

Lazarus started to brush her off the way he had done to Dr. Hancock but he stopped - not only would it not be right to do that to his wife but it would also be a guaranteed failure. She would not take no for an answer and she knew him too well to believe a lie. Matching her quiet tone, he said, "I've been seeing things… flashbacks to horrible events that have happened to us over the years."

"What sort of things?"

"Just injuries that we've all accumulated. Gory things."

"You're being evasive."

Lazarus squeezed his wife's hand, drawing her gaze to his. His eyes were mismatched - one a dull brown and the other a glittering emerald. It was a condition known as heterochromia and it was very useful in locking someone's full attention onto his stare. "Kelly, please… trust me this time. If I could tell you more, I would. I have my reasons for keeping this close to the vest."

Her expression softened, the annoyance at being kept out of his affairs slowly replaced by concern. "I do trust you. Just… let me help."

"You help just by being here."

"Then I'll leave it to you to tell me when the time's right." Kelly took a deep breath. "But don't think I'm not going to be worried about you."

⸙

"You saw it, didn't you?"

Samantha sighed, leaning back in her chair and crossing her legs. Her blue eyes gazed off into the distance and she looked rather serene, except for the dancing of one foot. Her glance shifted to the clock - it was nearly two in the morning, well after the birthday festivities had ended and everyone else had gone to bed. "Yes, Morgan, I saw it. We all did."

Morgan paced back and forth, hands buried deep in the pockets of his slacks. He looked good for his age but Samantha knew that the years were starting to catch up to him. He winced a bit as he moved, a sign that he recovered a little bit slower than he once had. The group's adventures took a toll on everyone but Morgan seemed to feel them a little more than everyone else.

Abruptly stopping, Morgan turned to face his friend. Of everyone in the group, he was closest to Samanth and the two of them were practically inseparable when it came to sharing concern over Lazarus. "Something strange is going on... and I feel like I should know what it is. I just can't quite put my finger on it!" Before Samantha could say anything, Morgan continued, "When I heard from my sister[3], she told me something important and I'm positive it had something to do with Lazarus. I can't figure out why I can't remember what it was."

"Have you asked Abby to help? She can probably whip up some spell that would get the memory back."

Morgan placed his hands on the back of a chair and sagged against it. "No... I guess I should. I haven't said anything to anyone but you. I just keep feeling uneasy about Lazarus."

"What does that mean?" Samantha looked at Morgan with a curious expression. "I thought you were just worried about his health or something... but your tone makes me think something different."

"I don't know what I mean," Morgan admitted. He gave a shrug and added, "All I know is I've avoided being alone with him."

A soft chiming sound made both of them turn towards a door that led from the meeting room into the monitoring area. Typically someone was assigned to keep track of the various cameras mounted on the exterior of the property and it was Morgan's turn. That explained his own late-night hours but Samantha had only joined him after waking up with an unsettled digestion brought upon by eating too many sweets.

Morgan entered the other room, prompting Samantha to ask, "What set off the alarm?"

"There's someone at the front door," Morgan replied. Samantha

---

3 A strange series of events detailed in volume 11.

stood up quickly and had joined him by the time he'd activated the speaker system that allowed him to converse with anyone on the exterior of the property. Samantha saw a thin young man looking anxiously at the plaque mounted on the front door. It read CRIMINALS OF THE WORLD BEWARE, FOR THOSE IN NEED ARE ABOUT TO RECEIVE... ASSISTANCE UNLIMITED!

"Mind telling me what you need at this hour, mac?" Morgan asked. His words made the young man nearly jump out of his shoes. The camera image was clear enough to reveal a man in his early twenties, dressed in a suit that was slightly too large for him... he looked like a kid playing dress-up in his dad's closet. With straw-colored hair and rather wide-set eyes, the youthfulness of his appearance was even more apparent.

"Sorry - I know it's late," the young man replied, looking around as if unsure where to address his words. Spotting the intercom mounted near the door, the stranger took a step towards it and his voice became much louder. "My name is Shane Fitzgerald and I need assistance."

Morgan sighed, running a hand through his hair. "Sam, you mind sounding the alarm? Wake up everybody and I'll escort Mr. Fitzgerald into the meeting room."

"You don't want to talk to him first? What if it's a gag and we don't need to disturb everyone?"

"I recognize the look in his eye, kid -- he's desperate. Whatever's brought him out here in the middle of the night, he thinks it's serious. Call it a hunch if you want - I'll take the blame if it doesn't pan out."

Samantha gave a nod and stepped from the room, hurrying to rouse the rest of Assistance Unlimited. For a moment, Morgan hesitated before speaking to young Mr. Fitzgerald. He was glad for the distraction from his concerns about Lazarus... he loved his friend like a brother. If not for Lazarus, Morgan would have continued down a dark path that would have inevitably ended with him bleeding out in a gutter. Lazarus had given him hope and pride... and, eventually, a family.

Sometimes families have secrets, he mused. *Maybe I should stop thinking about this as something you're keeping from us... and instead look at it as an opportunity to help you with whatever you think you have to handle on your own.*

CHAPTER III
YOUNG FITZGERALD'S PLEA

THE GROUP ASSEMBLED so quickly that Morgan assumed that many of them had already been awake when the call went out. Lazarus and Kelly, in particular, had come down wearing the same clothes they'd worn at the party - and he figured they had continued their conversation upstairs. He wondered if Kelly had gotten any information out of her husband but from the tight set of her mouth, he assumed she hadn't.

The meeting room was slightly chilly and Morgan was glad to see that Eun had brewed a fresh batch of coffee and was passing out mugs of java.

Fitzgerald had a cup of coffee, too, but he didn't touch it. Up close, he looked even younger than before - with just a few wispy hairs on his chin making Morgan think the boy had only recently begun shaving. His eyes were in continuous motion, looking from the members of Assistance Unlimited to the various unusual objects that lay on the shelves against the walls. Morgan saw the youth's gaze fall upon an urn that had once contained Princess Femi's immortal remains before moving on to a fist-shaped gem known as The Gem of G'vos. Eventually, Fitzgerald realized he couldn't stall any longer and he said, "I am sorry for waking everyone up."

Lazarus drew up a seat across the table from Fitzgerald. "Don't worry about that. Just tell us what brought you here."

With a shaky voice, Fitzgerald launched into his tale. At first, he kept his eyes on the table in front of him but occasionally he would look up, taking in the faces of those around him. He seemed to be intimidated by Lazarus and ended up looking mostly into Samantha's face as he spoke.

"I'm distantly related to the writer - F. Scott Fitzgerald," the youth revealed. Several people in the room were visibly moved by this admission - the author of *The Great Gatsby, Tender is the Night,* and *The Beautiful and Damned* had died back in 1940 of a heart attack and his work was still quite popular. Abby, in particular, was a devoted fan of *Gatsby* and had read the book four or five times. "As such, I've had a little bit of notoriety in Sovereign's literary circles... I fancy myself a poet, you see, and using the Fitzgerald name has opened a few doors for me. My actual surname is Glover."

Lazarus glanced over at Kelly, who was taking notes. His wife was seated beside The Black Terror and the two of them could not have looked more different: Bob was dressed in his leather uniform with a skull and crossbones emblem on the chest while Kelly was still wearing her casual clothing from earlier in the evening.

Kelly was adept at not only transcribing a person's words but including details that others might miss - for instance, Fitzgerald was not just nervous... he was borderline terrified.

Samantha had picked up on this, as well, and she reached out to squeeze the young man's hand. Color rose to his cheeks - a common occurrence for young males when they were in Samantha's presence. "You're safe here, Shane. This is the most secure building in the entire city."

Fitzgerald nodded and continued, "About six months ago a man came up to me while I was out drinking one night. He introduced himself as Mr. Potts and he said that he'd heard about me... he wanted to hire me to ghost-write a book for him. He said he'd give me the plot details and I'd write each chapter. He offered good money and I accepted. We started meeting monthly and he told me that his book would be a thriller about a man that was killing women and the police's attempts to catch him. He had the first chapter ready to go - or, at least, a description of the killer's actions. I had to flesh out the motivations and everything else. He was very... detailed. As the months passed and we had more meetings, it was always the same - he would arrive with another scenario in which the killer would murder someone. He was totally uninterested in what I came up with for the rest of the book. All he contributed were details about the crimes."

Eun glanced at Abby and muttered under his breath, "I think I see where this is going."

Abby barely suppressed a grin. Her brunette hair was pulled back into a ponytail and she looked like she was ready to go back to bed. She and Eun had been commiserating about their lack of sleep recently just prior to the meeting getting underway.

Fitzgerald added, "Eventually I stumbled onto a newspaper article from the city of Hancock - I spotted it while traveling. It described a series of murders that matched those that Mr. Potts had told me about, down to specific details. At first I thought maybe Potts had read this same article and used it for the book... but the dates didn't match up. He'd told me those details *before* the murders took place! I knew then and there, with absolute certainty, that Mr. Potts was the murderer! He'd had me writing down his exploits for some sort of perverse thrill - saving them for posterity in the guise of fiction!"

The Black Terror spoke up, pointing out, "And yet you're here... instead of at the police station."

"I thought about going to the authorities, of course, but when I went to the station, he was waiting outside... his face split into a leering grin. He knew! Somehow he knew that I'd discovered the truth and he was waiting for me! I turned and ran - and since then he's been following me, appearing at odd moments to let me know that he could kill me at any time. That's why I came to you! I need you to protect me."

"We'll make sure you're safe, of course," Lazarus said. "Do you have any physical evidence to prove that Mr. Potts is involved in this?"

"I have my papers - all the things that he told me, including things that I'm sure only the police would know!"

Lazarus leaned forward. "And do you have an address for Mr. Potts? Or a phone number? How do you contact him? Do you know his first name? Has anyone seen the two of you together? Because without any of that, the police might see you as a suspect… a madman that's imagined Potts. I can tell you this - he didn't follow you to this area. If he had, we'd have caught him on one of the monitors… and no one but you has stepped foot on this street since just past eleven."

Fitzgerald's eyes grew large and he looked desperately at Samantha, as if trying to will her into believing him. "I swear, I'm not a murderer! I'm not making any of this up! We met for the first time at the bar but I'm not sure if anybody would remember him - after that we met at my apartment each time. My landlady might have seen him. And I can describe him! He's short and kind of stoop-shouldered, with a long face and black hair. He wears expensive suits."

"Shane," Lazarus said and the young man's head whipped around. "I believe you. We all do… I'm just telling you that you made the right decision in coming to us and not the police. Without more to go on, they'd send you back home without even so much as an escort." Standing up, Lazarus continued, "You have a copy of the novel on your person?" When Fitzgerald nodded, reaching into his oversized coat to pull free a set of dog-eared pages, Lazarus added, "Morgan, will you please look over the text and see if you can spot any clues? Eun, I want you and Bob to go to Mr. Fitzgerald's apartment. Stake out the vicinity and see if Mr. Potts comes calling. Abby, I'll need you to use your magic to get a clear image of our mystery man and implant it in each of our heads so we can be sure to recognize him. Samantha, you and I will journey to Hancock City - that's where the murders took place and it stands to reason that our killer might live in the area."

Kelly looked up from her notes, asking a question with her eyes. Her husband nodded, silently informing her that he needed her to stay at headquarters and coordinate their efforts. Abby would also be staying nearby, given that her contribution to the hunt wouldn't take very long to accomplish and her role as warden at Tartarus[4] required her to avoid long trips away from the city.

All doubts that anyone might have had about their leader dissipated as Assistance Unlimited jumped into action - a mystery had a way of galvanizing their sense of unity.

---

4 The super-prison designed by Lazarus to house his most dangerous enemies for whom traditional jails would not be enough.

Kelly reached out and patted Fitzgerald's hand. "Let's find you a room, shall we?"

———∞∞∞———

ABIGAIL SAT CROSS legged on the floor, a lit candle dripping wax in front of her. Fitzgerald was across from her, looking uncomfortable. The room he'd been placed in was comfortable enough but with all the lights out and only the candle for illumination, it had taken on a sinister ambience.

"Is all this really necessary, Miss Cross?"

"Abby - just call me Abby. And I'm afraid it is. Do you believe in magic?"

"Not really. I'm Catholic."

Abby smiled, reaching up to pull her dark hair back behind her head. She performed one of those quick twists to tie it back with a small hair tie that often left young men confused by the speed and skill of the action. "Then you definitely should believe in magic. I mean, you accept that Jesus turned water into wine, right? That he rose from the dead? That sounds like magic to me."

"I suppose so," the young man grudgingly admitted. "I guess I never really thought of it that way."

Reaching out with both hands, Abby said, "Put your hands in mine and we can begin. It'll be painless, I promise."

Swallowing, Fitzgerald did as he was told. He was aware that his palms were sweaty and that his heart was hammering in his chest. Why did every woman associated with Lazarus Gray have to be so pretty? He'd always felt awkward around attractive females and here he was holding hands with one.

"Now, I need you to close your eyes and focus on recalling what Mr. Potts looked like - the more detail, the better. Keep thinking of him, no matter what happens. You'll hear me saying some strange things and you might feel a pressure in your head, that's my mind touching yours. I'll see the image and then pull back."

"You'll... see what I'm thinking?"

Abby resisted the urge to grin. "Yes... but don't worry. I've done this before. Nothing that pops into your head will surprise me and I won't judge you for it, either. Young men often have... interesting thoughts."

Fitzgerald screwed his eyes shut and desperately tried to rein in his mind. The fact that she'd actually voiced his fears only made it worse and all sorts of things rose up unbidden before his mind's eye: things about Abby, about other women he'd fancied and most especially about Samantha Grace.

Thankfully, Abby began the ritual just then and the youth's amorous thoughts began to dissipate. She was speaking strange words that he didn't recognize but which made the hair on the nape of his neck stand on end. He shivered as a cool breeze seemed to snake through the room and through the lids of his eyes he thought he detected the candlelight begin to flicker.

Mr. Potts appeared in his mind and Fitzgerald tried to recall every small detail about the man. Unfortunately, despite being a writer, the young man had always been a bit self-absorbed and he often took little notice of others. Even Samantha, whom he was already smitten with, was a series of body parts and an indistinct smile. If pressed, he couldn't have told you the color of her eyes or what kind of shoes she'd been wearing just moments before.

Slowly, an image of Mr. Potts began to form in his mind. Abby could see a man that appeared to be in his mid-forties; with jet black hair; a thin, almost gaunt face; sunken eyes; and a suit that looked almost as nice as the ones that Morgan favored. The man's shoulders rolled forward and his head was held low, as if it were trying to recede into his neck. As she looked at the mysterious figure, she saw his eyes rise to meet hers - it was almost as if Mr. Potts were staring back at her, aware that she was observing him. That was impossible, of course - this wasn't actually Potts, after all, but merely a memory. It didn't feel like Fitzgerald was doing this, though... and things took a turn for the worse when Mr. Potts actually began speaking to her.

As soon as the voice reached her, she tried to release her hold on Fitzgerald's hands and pull free of his mind but something held her firmly in place: something dark and malevolent... and all-too familiar. "Hello, Abby... it's been far too long."

"No," Abby said aloud, causing Fitzgerald to open his eyes. He felt her squeezing his hands almost painfully hard, her body beginning to twitch as if she were in pain. "It can't be you," she said again.

On a mental planescape invisible to Fitzgerald, Abby was watching in horror as Mr. Potts began to change, his form slowly altering in a cloud of mist. Within seconds, he wore a long red cloak that seemed to envelope his body completely. His face was hidden behind a red mask that left his mouth and ears bare. Atop his head a set of horns curved inward and Abby wasn't sure if they were part of the mask... or the man's skull. It was the terrifying visage of Doctor Satan, one of the world's most dangerous men.

She knew that the masked man's origins were uncertain - some claimed he was nothing more than a rich playboy that had turned to mysticism after becoming bored with his day-to-day life... others said that he was far older than that, having been born in the days when the Pharaohs ruled Egypt... and she had heard from a sorcerer in New Orleans that Doctor Satan was actually John Willard, Salem's deputy constable during that strange period in 1692 when witchcraft seemed to lurk around every corner in Massachusetts.

Abby didn't know which story - if any - was true and she wasn't sure she cared. Doctor Satan's villainous exploits had been foiled in the past by supernatural investigator Ascott Keane, the Atlanta-based Peregrine, and perhaps most notably by Assistance Unlimited. During one lengthy attempt to bring down Lazarus Gray, Satan had managed to briefly corrupt Abby herself, a period in her life that she had tried to bury deep in her psyche[5].

Satan tilted his head to the side, regarding Abby with undisguised amusement. "Do you ever think of me, Abigail? In the dark of the night, do you remember how I felt inside your brain, my fingers all twisted up in your soul?"

---

5 Volumes 2-4 of Lazarus Gray featured the Satan-Lazarus clash.

Abby snarled, her attractive features shifting as she remembered how violated he had made her feel. She thought him banished from Sovereign forever - and perhaps in some way he still was. That could explain why his crimes were conducted in Hancock... but then how had he met Fitzgerald in Sovereign?

Rather than asking him for answers to those questions, Abby 'pushed' at him with all the mental might she could muster. The apparition was blown apart though she harbored no illusions that it had hurt him - Doctor Satan's mocking laughter made that more than clear.

Suddenly Abby found herself sitting once more in Fitzgerald's room - and the poor young writer had been thrown by her attack on Satan, the physical energy having manifested itself in the 'real world.' Fitzgerald lay half on his side, blood oozing from one nostril. He looked at Abby with alarm as she scrambled to his side but relaxed when she began speaking.

"Shane, I am so sorry! I saw Mr. Potts - but he turned out to be someone else entirely and I attacked him. I didn't even think that you might be hurt by it!"

"It's alright.. really." Fitzgerald allowed her to help him to his feet before asking, "You said he turned into somebody else...?"

"Yes," Abby murmured. "And we better tell the others before they head out to look for clues. Doctor Satan is one of the most evil men that's ever lived!"

CHAPTER IV
THE WAXWORK MURDERER

"I DON'T GET it," Eun said. He moved through Fitzgerald's apartment, which was littered with scraps of paper, empty bottles of beer, and remnants of clothing.

The Black Terror was kneeling nearby, easily lifting the couch with one gloved hand. "Explain?" he asked.

"Abby found out that Potts is really Satan... so why are we going ahead and looking for clues in this pigsty? What's there to uncover?" Eun used the tip of his shoe to brush aside a stained white shirt, revealing a set of women's lacy undergarments. Apparently, Fitzgerald's troubles with women didn't prevent him from the occasional lucky night.

Setting the furniture back into place, The Black Terror stood up and turned to face his friend. Bob Benton was the team's science specialist with a focus in chemistry. He was also the group's strongman, with super strength and flesh that was dense enough to repel small arms fire. A taciturn warrior, Bob Benton was actually a pseudo-human grown in a plantlike pod by the government to become a super-agent known as The Black Terror. Implanted memories were given to him to help create a personality that would encourage him to fight for the USA. Garbed in a uniform adorned by skull and crossbones on the chest, he had been meant to strike fear into the hearts of America's enemies. He had done so but only after breaking free of the government's control and finding a home with Assistance Unlimited. Accompanied by his girlfriend Jean Starr and his young ward (and sidekick) Tim Roland, The Black Terror became the scourge of the underworld - and his tendency towards violence often set him at odds with his teammates. Eun, being a bit of a hothead, rather liked Bob's forthright nature. For his part, The Black Terror was quite fond of Eun, as well - though Eun's homosexuality was an aspect of Eun's life that they simply didn't discuss.

"We know that Doctor Satan is behind all this... but we don't know the *why* of it." Bob said. "Lazarus thinks we have no choice but to play along for now - Satan has engineered all this and it stands to reason that it's to manipulate us somehow. Besides, we have no way of tracking him -- Abby tried and failed after she had that mental encounter with him. Maybe we can draw him out this way."

"Great - so we're all setting ourselves up as bait for the world's worst criminal." Eun wandered into another room, vanishing from the Black Terror's sight. It was only a few seconds before Eun shouted, summoning the black-garbed hero to his side.

The Black Terror found Eun in Fitzgerald's bedroom. Near an unkempt bed was a strange shrine of some kind: an altar upon which was laying what appeared to be a wax sculpture of a nude young woman, her mouth opened wide and her back arched. For a moment, Bob was uncertain if the scene was meant to be one of sexual excitement or severe pain. After staring at the visage for a few seconds more, Bob came to the conclusion that it was the latter.

Eun moved closer to the sculpture, bending over so he could examine it. "The amount of detail is amazing... but why would Fitzgerald have something like this? It doesn't seem like the kind of thing that kid would be into."

"It's new." Bob pointed at the carpet. "This altar is heavy. If it had been here for any length of time, it would have created a severe depression. I don't think this has been here for more than a few hours."

"Oh my god," Eun said, taking a sudden step backward.

"What is it?" The Black Terror asked.

"Look at her arm."

The Black Terror followed Eun's gaze - there was a spot where the wax had been smudged and pushed aside. What was revealed was a small patch of human skin. This was no sculpture - this was an actual woman that had been covered completely in wax!

Bob reached, pushing his fingers into the wax and slowly peeling it away. With it came flesh, revealing glistening red meat beneath. The woman beneath was dead but it was still a revolting moment, filling both men with dread.

Eun spun about, hissing "Bob! Someone's in the front room!"

The Black Terror tensed, straining his ears. He didn't hear anything but he trusted Eun. "How many?"

"I only heard one person's footsteps." Eun took a few steps towards the door, pausing just beside it. "There could be more, I can't be sure."

Wiping the blood and gore off his fingers against the side of his pants leg, Bob slowly turned. "Then let's go see who it is."

THE THING THAT was waiting in the other room could scarcely be called human - not any longer. It was a man but his upper half had been twisted all around so that his back was now facing front. His neck had twisted once more so his face looked in the proper direction but his neck was an ugly shade of bruised purple and black. He wore no shirt, revealing flesh that had been gouged deeply by the lashes of a whip. His slacks were so stained with blood and muck that it was impossible to guess at their original color... and he wore no shoes, just torn black socks.

"Hello, boys," the mangled figure said, his voice sounding hoarse. "Or are those the wrong terms for you two? Neither of you are really *boys*, are you? One's a plant and the other is a Nancy Boy."

Eun tensed, ready to spring into action. For once, though, Bob was quicker - The Black Terror crossed the room in a couple of long strides, seizing the monster by its mangled neck. "Where is Doctor Satan?" Bob demanded.

To Eun's surprise, the backwards figure brushed aside The Black

Terror's grip with ease and followed this up by delivering a powerful blow that knocked the leather-clad hero on his backside. "Don't touch me like that, pal," the stranger warned. "Nobody does that to Twist - you got that?"

With a cry, Eun launched himself in the air, aiming a kick at his enemy's head. The villain threw a hand up and gripped Eun's ankle, hurling him into a wall.

"That's not nice, boys... not nice at all. Doctor Satan says he'll reward me if I kill one of you. I wonder how good he'll treat me if I murder both?" Twist started to approach Eun, who was groaning and holding the back of his head. "I'm going to off you first, Nancy Boy. Your kind makes me sick."

Twist reached down and grabbed hold of Eun's hair, using it to pull the man to his knees. He drew back his free hand, balling it into a fist with the obvious intention of driving it hard into the young man's face... but the blow never landed. A pair of leather-clad hands grabbed Twist's wrist and gave it a powerful yank, dislocating it with a loud popping sound. Twist roared in pain, losing his grip on Eun.

The Black Terror lifted Twist up above his head and then brought the monstrous villain down with a satisfying crunch onto the floor. Bob followed this up with a shattering kick to Twist's ribs.

Eun held up a hand and Bob backed off. The Korean-American knelt beside the groaning villain and tilted the man's head back so he could look him in the face. "Doctor Satan... where can we find him?" he asked and when Twist didn't answer quickly enough, he slapped the man's face, leaving a red handprint. "Don't make me again."

Twist grinned maliciously. "That bitch of yours - Abby? - she banished him from the city. He can only enter if he's inhabiting someone else's form. So if you're looking for Mr. Potts... he's real. But he's just a vessel for Satan when the good doctor needs to take a ride."

"Nice to know," Eun said before slapping an open-palmed blow to Twist's nose that broke it. "Now answer my question."

Sputtering blood, Twist coughed out the words, "He's closer than you know. I told you - he can come to Sovereign whenever he wants, all he needs is a ride."

Standing up in disgust, Eun looked at Bob and asked, "You want to do it?"

Twist craned his neck around to see a cruel smile on The Black Terror's face. "No, wait--" the criminal muttered, just before Bob raised a booted foot and drove it straight into the side of his head.

Eun shook his head. "We should take him and the girl with us. Maybe Abby can get more out of him than we could -- and if we can figure out who she was, we can contact her family."

Bob nodded but he looked troubled. "He said Satan's closer than you know. What do you think he meant by that?"

Eun shrugged. "Who cares? Typical Satan double-talk. I wouldn't worry about it."

SAMANTHA AND LAZARUS walked through the fog-enshrouded streets of Hancock, always staying just far enough behind their quarry to avoid detection. They had found Samuel Potts easily enough - something that rather surprised Samantha, who had assumed that Potts didn't actually exist. She'd expected to find that Potts was nothing but a false identity used by Doctor Satan. In fact, Potts was a retired military man that had specialized in field surgery. He had been married twice, with the first ending when his wife died of tuberculosis and the second in divorce. The man was a member of the local Optimists Club and had twice served on the local school board.

His reputation was sterling… aside from whatever connection he had to the supervillain, of course. His public persona made his current whereabouts rather surprising, however: he had led the members of Assistance Unlimited into a poor, crime-ridden part of town. He came to a halt beside a woman wearing far too much makeup and a rather tawdry dress that revealed her stockings and her bra straps.

"Eww," Samantha said, turning sideways so it looked like she and Lazarus were engaged in a private discussion. They stood close enough to give the impression that they might be lovers and Lazarus added to this appearance by letting one hand rest idly on her hip. "Satan's got to be in control of him right now - surely a physician would know better than to lie down with someone like *that*. She's got to be crawling with disease, if not with bugs."

Lazarus kept his opinion about the prostitute's hygiene to himself but he kept an eye on the way the woman leaned in and whispered something in Potts' ear. They linked arms and she led him towards an alleyway between a pharmacy that was closed for the night and a second-hand clothing store.

"This is it," Samantha hissed, pulling away from Lazarus and reaching under her skirt to pull out a 'pocket pistol.' She held it with both hands as she began slowly approaching the alley.

Lazarus reached up to the shoulder harness he wore under his coat, unholstering his .357 Smith & Wesson Magnum. "Stay quiet," he warned. "I'm not positive he's here for a murder."

"What else would it be—?" Samantha asked sharply, her whisper breaking off as her eyes widened. She saw the prostitution on her knees, her stockings rubbing against the filthy ground. Her head was bobbing as Potts' hands were entwined in her hair. She whirled about, color rising to her cheeks. She looked sheepishly at Lazarus and added, "He might be planning to kill her... *after*."

Lazarus gave a slight shrug and whispered, "Regardless, we need to speak to him and find out if he can help us track down Satan. If you don't mind standing guard at the end of the alley...?"

Samantha nodded and turned back around, obviously embarrassed by her discomfort. She held her gun at the ready as Lazarus stepped into the alley and spoke, using his most commanding voice.

"Samuel Potts! Raise your hands - now!"

The prostitute backed away so quickly that she fell on her rear end in a puddle of waste. Cursing, she wiped her mouth with the back of her hand and then scrambled up, running full tilt towards Lazarus and Samantha. Neither of them tried to block her path and the woman of the night vanished from sight within seconds.

Potts, meanwhile, was adjusting his fly and looking properly frightened. "Oh my god! There's no need for guns!"

Lazarus approached, the barrel of his handgun pointed directly at the man's forehead. "I hope you're right, Mr. Potts - but until you answer a few of our questions, I'm afraid we can't put them away."

"What is this about?" Potts asked, reaching up with a trembling hand to brush back a lock of hair that had fallen forward. "You're Lazarus Gray, aren't you? I would think this is a little beneath you, isn't it?"

"We want to know about your relationship with Shane Fitzgerald… and Doctor Satan."

Potts barely blinked at Fitzgerald's name but when Lazarus said Doctor Satan, a definite change came over the man. He no longer looked embarrassed or afraid - instead, his face was now twisted into a hateful expression. With surprising speed, he jumped at Lazarus, kicking out with one foot. The attack hit Lazarus in the wrist, knocking his gun against the brick exterior of the pharmacy. The impact caused the gun to go off but the bullet bounced off the wall and ricocheted off the ground.

Potts spun about and seized hold of a fire escape ladder. He was in the process of yanking it down when a bullet from Samantha's gun caught him in the shoulder and sent him cursing to the ground. He held his gun and whined like an injured dog, his eyes rolling up into his head and spittle flying from his lips.

Samantha rushed forward, stopping only when Lazarus held up a hand to keep her from getting too close to the thrashing form of Mr. Potts.

"What's wrong with him?" she asked. "That bullet can't hurt that bad."

"It's almost like a seizure or a fit -- I think it has more to do with Doctor Satan than your attack."

Once more, Potts reacted to the villain's name. His head snapped back and he turned towards the heroes, his lips pulling back into a rictus grin that showed the red of his gums. "Potts is just a vessel... weak and easy to overwhelm. He doesn't know the things I've had him do. He thinks they're just dreams, nightmares, fantasies." The voice that came from Potts' throat was not that of the man who had spoken to them just a moment before. This was deeper, huskier... it was the voice of Satan himself. "He and Fitzgerald are writing such a story, Lazarus... you'd like it. I think you'd find it *very* interesting. You really ought to read it." Potts' eyes rolled towards Samantha. "Then again, maybe you're the one that would find it most interesting. It's all about a fellow that thinks he's doing good things - but in the end, he's killing those around him. Murdering them in the most awful ways and they don't even know that it's him betraying him!"

Lazarus drove the barrel of his gun hard between the fallen man's eyes. Samantha gasped at the violence of the action and at the way her friend's entire body shook with rage. She felt a sense of awful certainty that Lazarus was about to murder a man right in front of her and she was too shocked to take action.

Then, the moment passed - Potts looked confused and frightened once more and Lazarus jerked the gun away, holstering it and turning away. With an unsteady voice, he told Samantha, "Bind him with some cuffs and I'll help get him into the car."

Samantha pulled a pair of specialized rubberized bands from a pocket - they had been designed by Lazarus and despite their appearance, they could hold even the strongest of men at bay. As she knelt and began to affix them to Potts' wrist, she asked, "Are we going to drop him off with the local police?"

"No -- I'm sure they'd find a mountain of evidence to convict him but he's an innocent." In a lower tone, Lazarus added, "A man can't be judged by what he's forced to do."

Samantha said nothing but she was afraid - she'd never seen Lazarus look the way he just had. It was almost like he'd been transformed into a stranger.

A dangerous one.

CHAPTER V
THE BOOK OF SATAN

MORGAN WATTS TOOK a sip of coffee, wishing it was a cup of brandy instead. He'd given up smoking and numerous other vices but he still imbibed from time to time... but never when he was working and that's what this business definitely qualified as. Reading this sick piece of work was almost enough to turn his stomach and he'd seen more blood and guts in his time to make him immune to most violence. Fitzgerald had a knack for crafting interesting characters with a sparse minimum of words, which made the killing scenes all the more intense. As the young man had warned, those parts of the story sparkled with vivid detail and knowing that they were inspired by real events kept forcing Morgan to look away from the page and give himself time to recover before diving back in.

What was even worse was the strange backstory to the overall narrative... the protagonist of the book was a killer, hiding in plain sight, pulling the wool over the eyes of even his closest friends and lovers. Through some bizarre means, the murderer had devised a way to revive some of his murdered victims - not out of guilt or an attempt at redemption but simply so he could slay the amnesiac victims over and over.

That part of the tale caused a tickle to form at the back of Morgan's brain...

"It is most strange, is it not? How some things can give us the deja vu?"

Morgan froze, his hand outstretched towards his coffee mug. He turned in his seat, looking at a most unusual individual. The stranger was dressed in a gaudy purple suit, a low-brimmed hat pulled downward in the front, partially obscuring a thin face. A feather, dyed the same monochromatic shade as its owner's suit, was fitted inside the hatband.

"Who the hell are you?" Morgan asked, his eyes narrowing. Nobody - absolutely nobody - simply waltzed into 6196 Robinson Avenue. This strangely dressed man had seemingly done just that.

"Just a humble investigator, mon ami." The purple-garbed man leaned forward with a flourish of his hand. "I am L'Homme Fantastique. It is an embarrassing name, I must admit… but I do try to be worthy of it."

L'Homme Fantastique. Morgan felt his jaw drop open. That was a name that all boys and girls in Sovereign knew… a sort of bogey-man that had haunted the city for longer than anyone could count. They said he lived in an ivy-covered mansion whose location shifted depending upon his mood. Some said he wasn't human at all but the spirit of a deceased gambler, cursed to roam the Earth in an attempt to make good on his many sins.

Morgan started to rise but he stopped when L'Homme Fantastique held out a gloved hand containing an envelope.

Morgan accepted the offering, looking at it and seeing that Lazarus Gray was written across it in flowing script. "What is this?" Morgan asked, though he remembered enough from the stories of his youth to suspect what it was: an invitation to play a game, one that could offer redemption or death to the invitee. "This can't be real," Morgan muttered. He looked up, ready to accuse this uninvited guest of playing some sort of twisted game - perhaps, he thought wildly, it was related to Doctor Satan and his penchant for trickery.

L'Homme Fantastique seemed to know what he was thinking, however, for the strange man said without prompting, "I have no affiliation with the foul Doctor… in fact, it is men like he that I have spent more than one lifetime fighting against. I am not the Almighty, however, and I know that my judgment can be flawed… so I give all the chance to prove their innocence. You will give that to your employer?"

Morgan looked down at it, marveling at the notion that L'Homme Fantastique was apparently real… and he wanted to give Lazarus the opportunity to prove his guilt or innocence. When he looked back up, L'Homme Fantastique was gone, having vanished as mysteriously as he had appeared.

CHESTER WINIFRED CHEWED his bottom lip and nervously drummed his fingers on the top of his desk. He was an accountant whose chief business lay in making sure that certain activities remained 'off-books.' He kept two sets of books for almost all his clients - one for the prying eyes of the law and the other that lay out the full breadth of his clients' doings.

Business had been good these past few years, allowing Chester's bank account to balloon alongside his waistline. He had an attractive home, a doting wife, two round-faced children, and a young mistress that he kept up in an apartment downtown.

Unfortunately, Chester had gotten sloppy. He'd accidentally turned over the wrong set of legal papers during a recent inquiry from the police… it was a terrible mistake, one that had led to tense moments for his client and more than a few sleepless nights for Chester. Now it was time for the two of them to come together and determine what the future of their relationship would be…

The door to the office opened without preamble and Chester caught a glimpse of his terrified secretary, a pert young blonde with big breasts, staring at him with wide eyes.

Chester looked at the person that had entered his office. He saw a graceful, childish figure wearing a black velvet suit with a lace collar and with hair curls waving about the handsome, manly little face, whose eyes met his with a look of pure malevolence.

The dwarfish gangster wore what was known as a Fauntleroy suit and as a result some had taken to calling him Little Lord Murderboy, a reference not only to his fashion choices but to his reputation for killing indiscriminately. His real name was Ty Barron and Chester just hoped and prayed that he wouldn't slip up and call him Murderboy. Rumor had it that he'd once cut a man's tongue out with a rusty spoon for having used that name.

Murderboy walked up to a chair and hefted himself up into it with a small amount of effort. When he was situated, he glared at Chester and asked, "Well? What do you have to say for yourself?"

Chester flinched, despite the fact that the other man's voice was somewhat high-pitched, reminding the accountant of the Munchkins from that Oz movie. "It was a mistake, that's all. I'm sorry, Mr. Barron. It won't ever happen again."

Murderboy reached into the folds of his outfit and withdrew a small handout pistol, the sort that ladies sometimes carried in their purse. On him, though, it looked full-size. "I know it won't happen again, Chester. I'm going to 'fire' you? Get it?" He cackled and Chester swallowed hard, thinking not of his wife and children but of his mistress.

The accountant threw up both hands and pleaded, "No! Don't! I have something that will make it all up to you! I swear!"

"Really, Chester? That seems unlikely but what the hell?" Murderboy pointed the gun at the ceiling and shrugged his shoulders. "Let's see it - but I warn you: if you try to pull out a piece from that desk of yours, I'm gonna shoot your balls off."

Chester slid his chair back a bit and slowly pulled open the center drawer of his desk. Keeping an eye on Little Lord Murderboy's weapon, he reached inside the desk and slowly withdrew a dusty old book bound in cracked leather. "One of my clients managed to snag this one - the old Boyd Building was demolished and a box of books were pulled from the remains. Most of them ended up in the hands of Assistance Unlimited but my client used to do work for El Demonio[6] and recognized that this one might be of interest."

"Demonio?" Murderboy sniffed. "The guy with the luchador mask?"

"He had an interest in the supernatural," Chester replied, trying to justify his belief that this book would be worth gaining Murderboy's

---

6 The masked villain tormented Assistance Unlimited in volume seven.

forgiveness.

"Yeah, yeah... I've heard how tough he was. All I can say is: if he was all he was cracked up to be, how come he's been in Tartarus the past four years?" Murderboy gestured for Chester to slide the book over to him. "Let me see what you got. It better be good!"

Murderboy looked at the cover with a frown and then began turning the pages. His expression shifted as he began to study some of the words that had been scrawled within. The handwriting was shaky and the ink had blotted in places, making it difficult to fully decipher... but it seemed to be a written description of a location in nearby Hancock City. It went on to detail what was buried under the ground at this site and what could be with it once it had dug up.

"Do you see what I mean?" Chester asked, feeling hope for the first time since Murderboy had entered the office. "That's something you can use, isn't it?"

Not answering, the diminutive criminal turned back to the inside cover. There was an image scrawled there, a crude drawing of a horned man's head and shoulders. "What's this?" Murderboy asked, holding up the image for Chester to see.

The accountant shrugged his shoulders. "Supposedly the whole stash belonged to a lunatic called Doctor Satan... a few years back Lazarus Gray kicked him out of town and that's why the books were still there when the place was demolished. I don't think anybody knew that except for Demonio's people."

Little Lord Murderboy shook his head, sending his curls dancing. "Some people are strange."

Says the grown man in the Fauntleroy outfit, Chester thought. He wisely kept the opinion to himself.

Murderboy closed the book and set it in the chair next to his hip. He regarded Chester and said, "You know, you're right... this book is worth your life."

Chester exhaled, visibly relaxed. "I knew you'd like it, Lord--" His eyes widened quickly, exposing the whites.

Murderboy's lips were now completely flattened, his nostrils flaring. "Go ahead and finish what you were about to say, Chester. Lord what?"

"I know your name, Mr. Barron. It was just a slip of the tongue." Chester started to stand, his hands and legs trembling. "I didn't mean any disrespect."

"You know why I dress like this?" Murderboy asked, glaring at Chester.

"I just figured.... you liked it?"

"I do but it's more than that. My mother used to read *Little Lord Fauntleroy* to me when I was a kid. I loved that book. These clothes were all the rage after it was published - every mom would dress her kid up like the character from the book. My mom eventually bought me a Fauntleroy suit for Halloween one year... I went out to get myself some candy and do you know what happened while I was out? Some bastard sliced my mom open from throat to crotch. She did whatever she had to take care of me, see? That included letting men in suits just like the one you're wearing come over and touch her with their disgusting hands. Only this one guy did more than touch her... he was still there when I got back while he was playing with the pieces of her, I grabbed a knife from the kitchen and I stabbed him thirty-two times. After that, I adopted this as my trademark, you see? I might have come from the streets but I was a nobleman in my mom's eyes and she was my Queen. I swore that I would rise to power, despite the fact that men like you would make fun of my attire."

"I wasn't--"

"Shut up!" Murderboy screeched. He sprang out of the chair so quickly that the leather-bound book toppled heavily to the floor. His gun spat out leaden missiles of death, each of which found a new home in Chester's head. The accountant was dead before his body toppled over in its chair.

Murderboy took several deep breaths before adjusting his curls and putting away his gun. Retrieving the fallen book, he stepped around the spreading pool of blood and exited the scene.

—∞∞∞—

DEMONIO GRUNTED AS he completed his two hundredth pushup, sweat dripping off his body. He sat back on his heels, gazing through the eye-holes of his Luchadore-style mask at the images he'd taped to the wall. They were pictures that he'd requested from the warden, showing the Mexican countryside. He had no doubt that he would see his homeland again but until then, these photos were the next best thing.

He stood up, his physique even more impressive than it had been when he'd entered Tartarus four years ago. When first captured, he had been stripped of his mask and an exhaustive attempt had been made to identify him. It had failed... he had long ago destroyed his birth certificate and murdered anyone that could have told of his past life... in the first few months, he destroyed pillowcases and clothing to fashion makeshift masks of his own - until finally his headgear had been returned to him.

The mask itself was ornately designed to inspire thoughts of monsters and demons, playing into the name he had given himself. Truth be told, El Demonio was an identity that he claimed after years of being called such by foster parents, teachers, and police officers. All of them had viewed him as a bad seed, a boy given to sin from a young age. After being insulted for so long, was it any wonder when he finally began to agree with their assessment? *Let them hate and fear me,* he had finally decided. *I don't need them. I need no one!*

For years, he had won every battle he'd waged. His criminal cartel was the most powerful in Mexico... but El Demonio had not been satisfied. He had become obsessed with the American vigilantes that seemed bigger than life, as if imbued with the supernatural: The Peregrine, with his glowing dagger; Leonid Kaslov, the Russian Superman; Gravedigger, with the rumors that she was part of some immortal line of warriors; and Lazarus Gray, for whom death itself was a frequent dance partner.

Seeking to gain this same sort of power, Demonio had begun investigating the occult. His mother had taken him to church as a youth and despite his pugnacious nature, he had taken her faith to heart. He believed in God… and in Hell. As such, he knew that there were objects of cursed nature loose in the world - and he wanted to have them. This eventually led him to a creature known as The King in Yellow and, through him, to Sovereign City. In the end, it had not been the fabled Lazarus Gray that had defeated Demonio… but rather, Eun Jiwon. The Korean-American's prowess was well-known to Demonio and he had relished the chance to fight him but the end result had left the crime-lord toppled from his empire and a prisoner.

"It's a shame that you wasted so much potential on a career of crime."

Demonio paused, his back to the cell door. He looked slowly over his shoulder, his eyes widening slightly beneath his mask. The man standing there should have, by all rights, looked ridiculous. Somehow the hombre managed to make the outfit work, however: tight white shirt with the American flag emblazoned upon it, tri-tiered hat, blue breeches, cloak, and buckled shoes. "The Fighting Yank?" Demonio asked, fully turning his body towards the hero. "To what do I owe this unexpected pleasure?" he asked. His voice was husky, with just enough rumble to it to make him seem both threatening and refined at the same time.

To Demonio's surprise, The Fighting Yank lowered his voice and cast a glance in both directions before speaking. It was as if the man was uncomfortable in these surroundings… but was he not a member of Assistance Unlimited?

"I've come to offer you freedom," the Yank whispered. "But it comes at a cost."

"Freedom always does, gringo."

"Something bad has infiltrated Robeson Avenue… and I'm afraid the only way to get rid of it is to rip it out. If I let you out, I need you to give me your word that you'll assist my friends and I."

Demonio grunted. "And what makes you think that I won't say whatever it takes to get out of this jail?"

"I think you're a man of honor under that mask… I think that under different circumstances, you could have become a hero to your people."

"You know very little of me," Demonio replied. "But nonetheless, I will give you my word… though I confess that I don't understand why you would need my help to deal with one of your group's enemies."

The Fighting Yank looked away once again and when he spoke, Demonio knew that the hero was deeply haunted by something. "I'm not sure what's coming around the bend… but I know it might be grim. You came close to defeating Eun in battle and now he's four years older… and you've had four years to live with the embarrassment of losing to him."

"You want me to fight Jiwon?"

"Him… and maybe others." The Fighting Yank's steely gaze returned to Demonio's and for a moment the two men's eyes were locked together. Demonio refused to look away, despite the feeling that he was being laid bare and that he was being judged, right down to his very soul. When the Yank spoke again, he accompanied his words with a nod of the head and the click of a key in the door's lock. "El Demonio… welcome to The Heroes."

CHAPTER VI
THE MAN IN THE MIRROR

HE HAD BEEN here so long that Dread Carcosa no longer held any terror for him. As he trekked across the sunburnt, cracked ground, a dead slayerbeast thrown over one tanned shoulder, he allowed his eyes to scan his surroundings, ever vigilant for any threat.

Twin suns were sinking in the distance, plunging the world into a strange sort of twilight. A cold wind blew off an inky black lake that was not far away and on the other shore lay a ruined city.

Creatures of bizarre sizes and shapes lurked in the seemingly abandoned houses that lined the cobblestone path upon which he trod. They watched him with glittering eyes and he heard their muted whispers. He was well-known to these beasts and all avoided him, having long ago concluded that it was better to toss and turn with hungry bellies than to risk death by confronting him.

He strode to the shores of the lake and he read a familiar wooden sign that had been driven into the moist earth. The words painted upon its surface were obviously drawn in blood: *Lake Hali, the place where my soul did die. All hail The Tatterdemalion King.*

Whomever had written those words was long gone and he'd stopped giving any regard to who they might have been. Instead, he tossed the corpse into a wooden boat that he'd built by hand, using scraps of wood that he'd scavenged in this terrible landscape. He jumped in, grabbing hold of the oars, and for just a moment he saw himself reflected in the dark waters: his skin was much darker than it had been upon his arrival and his physique was now hard and thin without an inch of excess fat but his eyes remained filled with an inner fire. He had not been broken by Carcosa and he felt certain that he never would... he had friends and a home and a lover waiting for him on the other side and eventually he would find a way back to them.

Until then, he simply had to survive.

He settled in and began to row across Lake Hali, his mismatched eyes fixed on his objective: a large tower that he called home. One of his eyes was a dull, ruddy brown and the other was a glittering emerald in color... and they were infamous in this dread dimension. When the evil ones spotted those eyes gleaming in the night, they turned and fled.

The wise ones did, anyway.

HE GUTTED THE slaybeast and had it for dinner, staying indoors during the most stygian hours of the night. The wind howled like a living thing, a desperate lost soul crying out for help.

He was reminded of a person - an entity - that he had first encountered upon arriving in this awful place. She introduced herself as Carmen and said that she was one of many lost souls trapped in Carcosa... but she had said more than that, too: *"Most of them go mad after they're here for long enough. There are days that I forget who I am, too. Maybe I'm not Carmen. Maybe I killed her when she came here and I absorbed her memories. I might just be a ghost of who she was."*

That conversation sometimes haunted him in the evenings. Was he just a ghost, too? Or was he a denizen of this realm that had merely adopted the identity of a human man? In the end, it didn't matter. Thinking of home kept him going and he refused to surrender the belief that he was real and that he was going to be reunited with his friends someday.

After enjoying his meal, the warrior lay down under a fur blanket, his back against the smooth, cool surface of the wall. He was facing the door in this fashion, a crudely formed knife held tightly in one hand. He was a hero and has risked his life many times since coming to Carcosa to try and aid those in need… but as Carmen had once said, most of them went mad after a brief time in this place. Some ran off into the night, never to be seen again… others had to be stopped more permanently before they did themselves or others harm.

Sleep finally creeped upon him and crouched, letting its warm embrace slowly enfold him. He drifted off, thoughts of Robeson Avenue drawing a smile upon his slumbering lips.

CHAPTER VII
HORRIBLE TRUTHS

ASSISTANCE UNLIMITED ASSEMBLED for lunch the next day in what had once been the hotel's banquet room. Where once the local Rotary Club had held their meetings and lavish parties had been thrown, the heroes of the city now piled their plates with food prepared by the group's part-time chef. The men and women gathered around two circular tables, while Lazarus stood at a podium facing them. He had eschewed taking lunch, choosing instead to spend a bit of time alone with the invitation from L'Homme Fantastique. Now he was back, envelope in hand.

Lazarus cleared his throat, attracting the full attention of his comrades. The children - Emily and Zeke - sat together at their own table, giggling over some shared joke. Even they fell silent, however, when Lazarus began to speak.

"We need to take stock of our current situation - a number of events are ongoing and we have no way of knowing if they're related or not. Let's start with the events at Tartarus late last evening. Abby?"

Abigail, smartly dressed in a navy sweater with a plunging neckline and a form-fitting skirt, stood up, looking somewhat chagrined. "El Demonio is free." Seated nearby, Eun Jiwon shifted uneasily. All of them had heard the tale of his one-on-one confrontation with Demonio and how close it had come to going the other way. "Someone with access to the prison entered, disabled the security cameras, and then used one of the keys to open Demonio's cell door."

Samantha leaned forward and asked, "That means it had to be one of us… right?"

Abby hesitated slightly. "Yes -- and no. It had to be a member of Assistance Unlimited but not all of us are here, nor did all of us attend the birthday party, remember?"

This time, it was Bob that spoke up. "Wait a minute - you're not accusing The Heroes of this, are you?" The Black Terror had joined The Fighting Yank, The Golden Amazon and Olga Mesmer in forming the aptly-named Heroes group. He split his time between Assistance Unlimited and The Heroes and both groups were considered part of the same greater organization. "The only reason they weren't at the party was because they were busy on a case - I heard that from The Fighting Yank himself and you know that guy rarely lies."

"Nonetheless," Abby replied, "they aren't answering the phone this morning and the actions of everyone in this room can be accounted for."

Samantha poked at her food with a fork before saying, "Well… there is one other person that might be capable of pulling it off. Eidolon."

Abby answered that quickly enough, having already suspected that someone would accuse her former lover and teammate. "I made contact with Jakob about an hour ago. He's in Paris right now and has been for the past two weeks."

Bob looked ready to argue the point further but Lazarus spoke up, saying, "It was either one of The Heroes or we have a major breach in security. Bob, would you mind taking a trip to their Manhattan HQ and looking into their role in this? I'd like Morgan to go with you."

"Of course," The Black Terror agreed. He glanced over at Morgan, who gave him a wink and a nod. "Is it fine if Tim comes along, too?"

"If you like." Lazarus gestured for Abby to proceed.

"In addition to the prison situation, Lazarus asked me to do my best to find out all I could regarding the poor girl found in Fitzgerald's apartment and the man called Twist. The young lady was named Abigail Wright and she was a willing participant… she was part of a satanic cult based in Hancock and she volunteered to be a sacrifice." Seeing the looks of disbelief and shock on her friends' faces, Abby added, "She had a change of heart at the last moment but by then it was too late. As for Twist," she said, quickly changing direction to get away from the discussion of the dead girl, "he's exactly what he appears to be: a sick pervert that's been physically altered by Doctor Satan. He's completely loyal to the Doctor and he was able to give me an address for where he sometimes met up with Satan. Potts wasn't even able to give us that month."

"So Fitzgerald is just a patsy, too? His role in all this was simply to draw us in?" Eun asked.

"As best as we can tell, Satan was just playing with him - much like how a cat will torment a mouse. The fact that Fitzgerald eventually came to us was a bonus," Abby answered.

"Thank you, Abby," Lazarus said and the pretty brunette returned to her seat. "That brings us to this --" he held up the envelope inscribed with his name. "Somehow , L'Homme Fantastique was able to get into and out of our home without being seen by a single camera."

"Maybe he freed Demonio, too," Kelly said and a few people nodded in consideration.

"We can't rule that out," Lazarus admitted. "As most of you are aware, stories about this L'Homme Fantastique character go back pretty far... overall, he's not considered a hero or a villain but rather a figure that has a particular sort of honor. He allows men and women who are accused of crimes the opportunity to fight for their survival via games of chance. The fact that he has challenged me indicates that he sees me as a figure of great curiosity and, potentially, someone that needs to be removed from Sovereign for the good of the community."

"What does the letter inside actually say?" Kelly asked, her concern for her husband evident in her features.

Lazarus slid a small folded piece of paper from the envelope. He opened it and read its contents aloud:

"Monsieur Winthrop/Gray,

Greetings! It is a matter of honor to which I must now write to you. It has come to my attention that your esteemed reputation may have been attributed to you in error. Deceptions and lies should be the coin of your enemies, not yourself. I ask that you put your affairs in order before the 18th of this month so that you and I may meet in private at 335 Kreecher Avenue. Be prepared for an evening of gamesmanship.

Failure to comply with the directions given above will lead to severe repercussions.

Sincerely, L'Homme Fantastique"

Silence descended upon the room, as even the children had ceased their playing. It was Morgan who finally asked, "What are you going to do?"

"Priority will be given to our pursuit of Doctor Satan," Lazarus replied. "We'll consider El Demonio's escape the second more important investigation. This L'Homme Fantastique... is by far the least of my worries."

"Can I look into it?" Kelly asked. When everyone glanced at her, she added, "I assume that the rest of you will be busy with the other stuff you mentioned and I can do some digging into the L'Homme Fantastique myths while I'm working at the museum. We have a whole department dedicated to local history, you know."

Lazarus nodded his assent. "Be careful - whether or not this character is the actual inspiration for all those stories, he's capable of getting in and out of here so he's dangerous. For all we know, he's Satan himself or at least another agent of his and this is all designed to split our focus."

"I met the guy, remember?" Morgan pointed out. "I believe it was really him. I think you should take this seriously, Lazarus."

"If he's actually L'Homme Fantastique, why is he coming after you, though?" Eun asked. "From everything I've heard, he only targets criminals."

"Maybe he knows something we don't," Morgan jokingly said but Samantha was close enough to him to see that the humor present in his voice didn't seem to reach his eyes.

"I'm serious," Eun said.

Lazarus held up a hand and said, "We really have no way of knowing - again, we don't have any hard evidence that L'Homme Fantastique is anything more than local folklore. Whomever this fellow is, he's just as likely to be working with Doctor Satan as he is to be the genuine article." With a decisive nod, the team's leader said, "I think we should finish our breakfast and then get started on our day's activities. Bob and Morgan will head to Manhattan to meet up with The Heroes, Kelly will begin looking into the background of L'Homme Fantastique and I'll lead Abby and Eun to the location that Twitch gave us. Samantha, you'll stay here and coordinate our efforts." Pausing for a moment, he added, "And everyone - be careful."

L'HOMME FANTASTIQUE OPENED the door to his private sanctum and immediately sensed that something was amiss. The sanctum's location was just outside of the Sovereign city limits, in a little unincorporated no-man's land known locally as Hobb's Row. The tiny community consisted of a hardware store; a small shop that sold both groceries and live fish bait; a dive bar; and a dozen or so small houses. It was usually quiet here and the residents kept to themselves -- there were good reasons why most of them eschewed living in the city, after all.

It was the perfect site for L'Homme Fantastique, for there were few people to try and monitor his comings and goings. Given his penchant for purple attire, it was not easy for him to move about undetected, even with his skill at hiding to the periphery of men's senses - thus, he was appreciative of the mind-your-own-business mentality of his neighbors.

On this morning, however, he knew that someone had trespassed on his property. The door was never left unlocked but it swung open easily at his touch today… and there was the smell of burning sulfur in the air. This odor was often known by another name - that being brimstone.

The interior of the room was swathed in darkness but he knew the interior like the back of his own hand. The furnishings were sparse, consisting mainly of a large wooden desk, a comfortable chair and several bookcases filled with books and boxes of classic tabletop games.

There was only one light in the room - a lamp that perched on the corner of the desk - and it was not currently illuminated. Despite the darkness, L'Homme Fantastique could discern the silhouette of an unusual figure sitting at the desk: male by the width of the shoulders, he guessed, and wearing some sort of cloak. Atop the man's heads were what appeared to be horns that curved up and back towards the skull.

Suddenly the lamp's bulb flared to life, momentarily blinding the apartment's owner. When his vision cleared, L'Homme Fantastique was staring at one of the most infamous figures in the world - the crimson-clad form of Doctor Satan.

"You've kept me waiting," Satan said, smiling as he leaned back in the chair. He folded his hands over his midsection and regarded L'Homme Fantastique like a boss weary of constantly having to reprimand the same employee time and again. "I've been here since about three in the morning. You keep odd hours."

L'Homme Fantastique approached the desk, coming to a stop just in front of it. "This is not your home, monsieur. You are an unwelcome guest."

Satan pointed a finger at the purple-garbed man. "Why do you have such a strong accent if you've lived here for over a century?"

The Frenchman swept his hands across the desktop, sending papers and the lamp flying. The bulb in the lamp shattered upon impact with the wall, plunging the room back into a stygian blackness. "Do not presume to taunt me, Doctor Satan! I have looked into the eyes of your namesake and I have not been found wanting!"

The red-garbed man rose slowly from his seat - in the darkness, L'Homme Fantastique could barely make out the smile that curled the villain's lips. "You and I both have an interest in Lazarus Gray... but I staked my claim earlier than you. So I'm asking you kindly to back off."

"Ah, mon ami, I am afraid I cannot do that. Once the invitation has been issued, it is out of my hands. I have rules to follow."

"Oh, yes... that 'patron' that you supposedly serve. I've never quite understood how it all works," Satan said, slowly walking around the desk to stand face-to-face with L'Homme Fantastique. The villain's cloak made a swishing sound as he moved. "Are you all about justice… or playing games? I don't see how the two have much in common."

L'Homme Fantastique's hand shot out and gripped Satan by the throat, applying enough pressure that the villain was suddenly gasping for breath. "My secrets are my own. My patron, as you call her, has decreed that I cannot take a life without giving them the chance to earn their freedom… but that does not mean that I cannot deliver great pain that falls just short of murder. Do you understand my meaning?"

Satan swept a clenched fist upwards, catching the Frenchman's wrist and knocking it away from his throat. "Don't threaten me - I know more about pain that you'll ever be able to conceive of." Turning so quickly that his cloak momentarily flew up and obscured L'Homme Fantastique's vision, Doctor Satan raised his voice and bellowed, "There's no peace between us! Kill him!"

The walls to the apartment were suddenly rent asunder by gunfire - L'Homme Fantastique realized in the split-second before he dove for cover under the desk that Satan must have had men stationed in the apartments on either side of his own… plus more were hidden outside. For a moment, the Frenchman wondered how the vile Doctor would avoid being killed in the barrage of bullets but a quick glance into the gloom that was now being lit by sunlight streaming in through the bullet holes told him that Satan had somehow pulled off one of his famous disappearing acts. The villain was nowhere to be seen, leaving L'Homme Fantastique to face a seemingly certain death.

Unfortunately for the men outside, L'Homme Fantastique was no normal fellow. He had stared death in the face too many times to count and always he had managed to emerge unscathed.

The storm of gunfire continued for nearly thirty seconds but it seemed like an eternity to the man under the desk. Several bullets struck the wooden frame that shielded him but he was unharmed when the assault suddenly ceased. Smoke drifted across his vision and he heard voices outside, conversing in low tones. They were debating whether or not they should enter the apartment to verify that he was dead.

L'Homme Fantastique crept out from under the desk, catching

glimpses of movement through the walls, which now resembled cheddar cheese because of the number of holes. The men appeared to be wearing dark suits with cloth masks over their faces. When he eventually got out of this, he would track them down - each and every one of them.

He snatched up a silver letter opener, knowing that it was sharp enough to slit a man's throat. He backed up against the rear wall, his eyes on the door. They were approaching and he knew that one of them would kick it open in seconds. He looked down, eyes quickly examining the floor - and he then stamped the heel of his left shoe down hard on a small, barely-noticeable crack in the wooden floor. The action caused a hidden spring to activate and part of the floor dropped open, revealing a ladder.

L'Homme Fantastique quickly clambered down, holding the letter opener in his teeth. He replaced the section of floor, sliding it back into place just as the door to the apartment was thrown open. He heard the sounds of their confusion as they realized that the apartment was empty and for a moment he considered bursting up into their midst and seeing how many he could defeat before one of them finally got him with their bullets. Thankfully, he was not a man given to impulse -- if he was, he wouldn't have lived as long as he had, his patron's grace notwithstanding.

He had built a hidden tunnel that eventually exited next to the site where one of Sovereign's storm drains opened onto Robbie Pond. Assuming Satan's soldiers were skilled enough to find the hidden trapdoor, they would be in pursuit soon - knowing that he had no time to waste, L'Homme Fantastique hurried down the tunnel. It was pitch black but the tunnel was small enough that there was no chance of getting lost - it ran in one direction only.

Moments later, L'Homme Fantastique came to a door which opened with a groan after he applied pressure with his shoulder. The roaring sound of water cascading from the nearby pipe reached his ears and he took a few seconds to catch his breath.

Satan wanted Gray all to himself... but that simply wasn't going to happen. Lazarus had to be given the chance to prove his innocence - and L'Homme Fantastique would be there to act as judge, jury and, if necessary, executioner.

CHAPTER VIII
COME UNDONE

MORGAN EXITED THE car, quickly falling into step with the much bigger man at his side. The Black Terror wore his full vigilante gear, making him look quite strange alongside the dapper-dressed Mr. Watts. Given that this was Morgan's first trip to The Heroes' Manhattan headquarters, he dropped back a step so his taller companion could lead the way.

Ahead of them was a four-story brownstone, situated between two smaller versions of itself. The building on the left bore a brass plate near the door that read 1299 Ferguson Ave. while the one on the right had a similar plate reading 1301 Ferguson Ave. The larger building in the center was missing its address label and Morgan felt a pang of amusement at that fact, considering that thirteen was generally held to be such an unlucky number.

There was no buzzer and Morgan watched as Bob simply approached the front door and opened it - it was neither locked nor latched. Morgan saw that the foyer was dark, illuminated only by light that came in through the open door. He saw a set of stairs that led upward and a pair of closed doors on the first floor. Stepping inside, he noted a list of tenants posted on the wall - according to the marquee, the first three floors were empty, while the fourth was simply labeled THE HEROES.

The duo began to ascend the stairs and Morgan took note of the fact that despite this being such an old building, there were no creaks to be heard. Nevertheless, he had a feeling of being watched and he suspected that the residents of this place knew full well that they were receiving visitors.

They bypassed the second and third floors, stepping onto the top level. Morgan noticed that there were four doors on either side of the stairwell, all of which were closed, and a single door that lay directly in front of the stairs... this door was open, revealing a circular table, heavy black drapes, a lit fireplace and a large American flag that hung from a golden stand.

The Black Terror led the way into this room, Morgan close at his heels. The elder member of Assistance Unlimited let his eyes fall upon the chairs arranged around the table... There were six of them and on the back of each was a symbol of some kind. The corners of his mouth twitched as he realized that he recognized four of these symbols - one of the chairs bore a skull and crossbones, just like the one that Bob wore on his chest. Another of the chairs featured a small American flag that appeared to be flickering in a breeze - this matched the image that The Fighting Yank had emblazoned on his white shirt. A third chair featured a golden sword that was plunged through a globe representation of the earth. Morgan was certain that this was a visual reference to The Golden Amazon, the powerful woman that had served as both friend and foe in the past. The next chair bore an image that showed a pair of eyes, outlined with a sort of pulsing energy. This chair obviously belonged to Olga Mesmer, who had pretty much put this grouping together from Morgan had been told...

The final two chairs, however, gave both men pause. Morgan glanced at Bob and could tell that he hadn't expected to see these two symbols, either. On one was a blue-colored flame... and on the other, most disturbingly, was a stylized image of a demon's face.

"El Demonio," Morgan said, a frown settling on his features. He drew his pistol, spotting the look of displeasure that Bob adopted at his action. "I know - I trust the Yank, too... but we barely know Olga and the Amazon's been an enemy as often as not. Teaming up with Demonio is enough to put anybody into the category of 'I don't trust them.'"

The door to the room, which had fallen to when Bob and Morgan had entered, now flew open. The Heroes - Olga Mesmer, The Golden Amazon, and the Fighting Yank stood there, alongside an unfamiliar man wearing a light blue tunic with a white collar-stripe and pants of a darker hue. Olga wore a light purple dress that ended at her knees while The Golden Amazon was decked out in white and yellow armor. Both women looked serious, as did the stranger in the blue tunic. The Fighting Yank wore an expression of grim resolve. El Demonio, on the other hand, was grinning beneath his mask, obviously thrilled at the shock evident in Bob and Morgan's eyes.

"Hola, Senor Watts. It is good to see you again," El Demonio muttered.

Morgan swung his pistol towards the masked villain but The Fighting Yank stepped between the men and raised a hand. "Put that away, Morgan. I know it seems strange but Demonio is one of us for now. There's a lot going on that you're not aware of."

"Well, you better start talking," Morgan replied, "because that guy's a stone-cold killer and if you've gone so far as to get a damned chair with his symbol on it, that's seriously messed up."

The Black Terror reached out and touched the barrel of Morgan's handgun. He pushed it downward and said, "Let the man talk, Morgan. If we don't like what he has to say, I'll personally clean his clock. Fair?"

Morgan nodded sharply, taking a step back.

Olga gestured towards the table and said, "Why don't we all have a seat? I'll bring in a spare for you, Morgan."

"I'm fine standing."

The rest of the group sat in their assigned seats and Morgan noticed that The Amazon and Bob were whispering something to each other. If the rest of The Heroes had been compromised somehow, was the same true for Bob? He'd had a fling or something with The Golden Amazon once before - and he'd almost turned against Assistance Unlimited when Eidolon had gone rogue.

Morgan tried to shake free of the paranoia. This was The Fighting Yank, after all - the guy was practically a saint. If he had Demonio here, surely there was a good reason for it.

As if on cue, The Fighting Yank stood up and began to speak. Though his words were addressed to everyone in the room, he looked directly at Morgan the entire time. "I'm glad that it's you that came with Bob... you see, none of this would be possible without you. Your sacrifice is what's given us the opportunity to see behind the proverbial mask." Morgan started to speak up but The Fighting Yank pressed on. "Three months ago, Morgan, you sent me a letter. I know that you don't remember it... because it wasn't quite *you* that sent it."

"What the hell--?" Morgan exclaimed.

"Stay with me," the Yank pleaded. "I promise it will all make sense in the end -- though even then, it's going to be hard to believe." When Morgan gave a grudging motion for him to continue, the Yank said, "Lazarus Gray hasn't been himself for quite some time. I think it goes all the way back to the King in Yellow affair[7]... when he made it back from Carcosa, he was a little more demonstrative emotionally... and he's gotten more so over time. He's more affectionate to his family, quicker to anger, more willing to tiptoe along the line of morality."

Morgan thought about his own concerns and found his anger starting to subside, replaced by a cold, gnawing kind of fear that start that started in the pit of his belly and then burrowed its way upward into his heart.

"A few years ago, Lazarus and Gravedigger began sharing information about their cases. That's how Lazarus discovered the Drake Island cloning program."

Morgan felt like he'd just received an electric shock. He literally swayed on his feet and had to grab hold of the back of Bob's chair to keep from falling to the floor. Images suddenly flooded into his mind - clear tanks containing the nude bodies of his friends, floating in some sort of strange fluid... even his own body had been there--!

Bob rose to help his friend but the touch of The Golden Amazon froze him in place. "Let the Fighting Yank continue," she whispered. "Morgan isn't being harmed - if anything, we're helping him."

The Fighting Yank continued once it was clear that Morgan had regained control of himself. "Lazarus warmed to the idea that Assistance Unlimited was a family - and this took even deeper hold after the birth of his son and Samantha became a mother. Not wanting to face the

---

7   Volume seven!

inevitability that one or more of you would die in the line of duty, he decided to use the cloning process to 'protect' you. When one of you died in the field, he revived you... and because he knew that knowledge of his actions might cause some of you to leave the group, he took extreme measures whenever one of you stumbled onto the truth. He killed you, Morgan. Multiple times. And it wasn't just you. In his mind, he's doing it to protect his family... but it's a dangerous sign of a sickness, Morgan. And it's going to keep getting worse. If he's willing to murder his friends to cover up his actions, what else would he stoop to?"

Morgan's mouth opened and closed several times before he managed to stammer, "I remember it. I remember him killing me. But -- how? I recall him saying that the clones' memories of their deaths wouldn't be there... that we'd only remember up to the point where we would cloned."

"We suspect that the process isn't as clearly-defined as he might like to believe," Olga answered.

Morgan turned suddenly to Bob and asked, "There wasn't a copy of you in the tanks. Is it because you're not totally human?"

Bob shifted uncomfortably. "I helped him with the process." Seeing the look of horror on Morgan's face, he quickly added, "He needed my expertise as a chemist to make sure the chemical ratios were correct. He made it sound like it was a last-case scenario... if one of you died in the line of action, we could revive you. I had no idea he was doing all of this... that you guys had died multiple times. You have to believe me! It wasn't until your letter arrived here that I began to learn the full story."

Morgan pointed an accusatory finger at Bob, asking, "Wait a minute - you've *known*? Even if it's only been for a few months, you've *known*... and you didn't tell any of us?"

"We've been taking our time, Morgan," The Fighting Yank said, trying to soothe the man's rising anger. "We wanted to verify what was in the letter... and then we wanted to have evidence for when we finally confronted the rest of Assistance Unlimited... and if they didn't believe, we had to be prepared for a fight."

"A fight," Morgan murmured. He looked at Blue Fire and El

Demonio. "That's why they're here. You're recruiting forces."

No one answered for a moment - and when someone finally spoke up, it was Bob, who was not known for being a peacemaker at the best of times. "Nobody wants a fight, Morgan. When Lazarus assigned you to come with me, I called ahead and let them know we were coming. It seemed like the perfect time to start laying all this out. We don't know if Lazarus was affected by his trip to Carcosa or what... maybe it's not even really him... but he needs to be called out. He's not supposed to play God... he's deciding which of you lives and which of you dies. He *murdered* you, Morgan. And not just once, either."

"I want to see the letter," Morgan said abruptly. "The one I wrote and that I sent here. I want to see it."

The Fighting Yank nodded at Olga, who slowly rose from her chair and left the room. She returned seconds later with an envelope, the top of which had obviously seen the business end of a letter opener.

Morgan accepted the envelope and quickly pulled out the piece of paper inside. It was handwritten in his own script and was on a piece of official stationery. Their motto - 'Criminals of the world beware, for those in need are about to receive...' ended just above a logo reading ASSISTANCE UNLIMITED. The text below caused Morgan to unconsciously hold his breath:

Heroes,

I know this must seem very strange but you have to believe me - I've uncovered evidence that Lazarus has been doing terrible things. He's killed people - a lot of people. Including, unbelievably, myself. He has these machines... these tubes... he grows us new bodies and we never remember what's happened to us. I'm going to confront him tonight and see what he has to say. I thought about giving this letter to Samantha or one of the others here but he'd just kill them, too. I think your group might be the only hope... if you don't hear from me within a week of your receipt of this missive, you'll know that I've died and been reborn.

At the bottom of the letter was a drawing of 6196 Robeson Avenue, with the hidden room sketched out.

Morgan set the paper aside and looked around the room. Aside from El Demonio, the rest of the group seemed tense, as if they were waiting for him to make some important pronouncement. Morgan found that his mouth was dry and it took a moment for him to work up the strength to speak. "We need to tell everyone else - Samantha, Eun, Abby... Oh, god, he hasn't done this to Kelly, too, has he? His own wife?"

The Golden Amazon shrugged her shoulders and answered, "We don't know that for sure... to be honest, my first reaction to this was that it seems like a practical use of technology. I was convinced that it was the deception that was in the wrong... if your friends willingly agreed to be reborn upon each death -- and Lazarus was not the one killing them to keep his secret safe -- I would have no problem with this."

"Neither would I," El Demonio rumbled. "As for the deception... he is your leader and he has decided that none of you need to know. I don't care about that, either." He laughed coldly but fell silent when The Fighting Yank gave him a disapproving glare.

The Yank leaned forward, shifting his gaze to Morgan. "Everyone is out of the building right now, aren't they?"

"Lazarus asked Samantha to stay behind," Morgan replied.

"Then let's go pay her a visit and see if we can get into this secret lair of Lazarus's," The Yank replied. "I think Samantha's going to need to see the evidence before she believes us, don't you?"

Morgan nodded, his mind still reeling from the truth. Was he really prepared to call his best friend in the whole world a murderer and a liar? And if Lazarus refused to come clean... then what?

CHAPTER IX
SOMETIMES THE TRUTH IS WORSE...

KELLY CLOSED THE door to her office and slowly returned to her desk. She'd spent most of the past hour looking through the local folklore section, collating all the references to L'Homme Fantastique that she could find. She hadn't studied any of them at length, wanting to first acquire everything she could so that she could evaluate their usefulness at length.

Sitting down in her leather chair, she allowed her eyes to drift over the stacks of paper... until they fell upon a framed photograph of her, Lazarus and Zeke. Their life together was certainly not a normal one but she cherished it. When she'd first met Lazarus, she'd found a passionate soul lurking beneath all that icy exterior... but it wasn't until the past few years that he'd begun to show that passion more and more. There were times he was still enigmatic, of course, but there were other times when the emotion she'd see in his eyes or hear in his voice would bring her up short.

She knew her husband better than anyone but there were moments when he felt... different... as if he were not quite the man she had once thought him to be.

The King in Yellow.

A shiver ran down her spine as she thought of the strange entity that had nearly plunged Sovereign City - and, by extension, the world - into madness. Lazarus had been forced to journey Dread Carcosa, an awful other world of pure chaos. Against all odds, he'd come back to her... but things hadn't been quite the same. He'd told her what he'd seen on the other side and she didn't think that he was holding anything back in that regard but he'd become increasingly concerned with protecting the members of Assistance Unlimited. He spent long hours alone in his study, behind locked doors, doing whatever he thought was necessary to ensure that his family was as safe as possible.

With a sigh, she leaned forward and started to look through the papers. L'Homme Fantastique was a legend going back to nearly the city's founding - tales of a mysterious Frenchman with a penchant for games of chance, whose origins were as mysterious as the source of his reputed powers. He was able to come and go as he pleased, often knowing things that secretive men had confided in no one. Those that crossed his paths were always left changed - either they lost the game and their corpses were found soon after or they won, swearing off whatever sinful affairs had led them across L'Homme Fantastique's path in the first place. Those few survivors often became men of the cloth or philanthropists of the highest order.

There were various conflicting accounts of his true identity: in one story, he was not a singular man at all but rather a secretive group that sought to clean up Sovereign City - when one member would die, another would be elevated to take his place. Another tale claimed that he had fled France to avoid being imprisoned for some awful offense and that he had begun enacting his own form of justice on others to try and alleviate his own sin. The third, and most frequently recounted, claim was that the Frenchman had been a visitor to the United States, having accompanied General Lafayette on his tour of America in 1824... the nameless Frenchman had been brutally murdered during the stopover in Sovereign. His spirit had somehow been revived and ever since he had delivered his own form of retribution on the guilty.

"The truth, mademoiselle, always lies somewhere in the middle, don't you think?"

Kelly reacted with rather impressive speed. Not even bothering to look to her left - the direction from which the voice had come - she snatched open the bottom right-hand drawer of her desk and drew her Walther PP handgun. She had it pointed at L'Homme Fantastique before she'd even really locked eyes on him.

The purple-clad Frenchman sat in one of her guest chairs, his head tilted downward so that the brim of his hat obscured his features. The bottoms of his pants and shoes glistened with moisture despite the fact that it wasn't raining outside.

Holding up a pair of gloved hands, L'Homme Fantastique said, "There is no need for that, Mrs. Gray. As you can see, I am unarmed."

Kelly's eyes flicked to the still closed door and back again. "How did you get in here?"

"I was already here when you entered. I have the ability to, how should I say it? Remain unseen?"

"Like the guy in that H.G. Wells novel?"

"Not quite like that," L'Homme Fantastique answered. "More a matter of confusing your mind... it is difficult to explain." He leaned forward and, much to her surprise, he removed his hat and set it atop a pile of papers on her desk. She stared at his face, unable to believe her eyes... it was like someone had smudged a drawing: the impression of a human face was there but it was unclear. She couldn't tell the color of his eyes, the shape of his nose, not even the curve of his lips... it was all *partially wiped away*. "This explains it perhaps better than words - what I am doing to obscure my features, I am able to do something on a larger scale to hide my entire being."

"My husband told me about a man that was able to do something similar... The Darkling." Kelly lowered her gun, not sensing that she was in any immediate danger. "He said it was like putting a cloud of another person's mind."

"A cloud? Oui. I like that." L'Homme Fantastique exhaled slowly and Kelly got the impression that he was tired. "You are delving into my background? Why not ask me what you would like to know, since I am here?"

Kelly stared at the stranger for a moment longer, still amazed by his bizarre appearance. Finally shaking herself free of the spell she was under, she looked away and asked, "Okay... who are you, really? And why are you threatening my husband?"

"My actual name is unimportant but I can tell you that I came here not longer after Sovereign was founded. I was an agent of the crown, sent here in pursuit of a criminal. I found him... and then I committed the worst sin of my life. I accepted a payment to pretend that I had not located him. I was tired of being at the beck and call of my monarch, you see? I wanted to begin anew in this new land, as so many already had... and so I betrayed my morals and let a bad man go free. He killed and hurt many people because of my actions and I knew this. On my deathbed, I was saved from an eternity in Hell by the Greek goddess Fortuna." He laughed softly before continuing. "I know how it sounds, mademoiselle, but I assure you that it is true."

Kelly said nothing, having heard much stranger things during her time with Assistance Unlimited. It actually sounded not too dissimilar to Gravedigger's story, in which she had been judged by a powerful entity and charged with carrying forth its message.

Realizing that Kelly wasn't going to comment, L'Homme Fantastique continued, "She was not just the god of chance, you see... worship of Fortuna was also closely tied to the concept of virtue. Anyone can be virtuous when the fates are kind, you see... but when chance throws things in your path that can tempt or challenge you, how do you respond? Those are the moments that truly test a man's character. That's where I failed, oui? Fortuna gave me eternal life but told me that it would be my duty to test the moral center of certain people... men and women that could have gone down the path of righteousness but did not. Are they truly beyond redemption? Did they make their decision for their own benefit or for cowardice or for the greater good? That's what I find out. I play games with them but the game itself is of little importance. It's how they react to my test, how they choose to comport themselves. Do you understand?"

"I think so... but I don't see why you're looking to test Lazarus. He's not a perfect man but he's walked the side of justice for as long as I've known him. You're not trying to hold his actions as a member of The Illuminati against him are you? He was unaware of their true nature and he's atoned for those many times over!"

"You are a good advocate for your husband, Mrs. Gray... but no. I am concerned with crimes of a much more recent nature. I am afraid that you are unaware of them."

"Enlighten me."

"I shall do so… but first, may I tell you why I am here now? In your office…?"

"Go ahead."

"I was attacked by minions of Doctor Satan - he was staking a claim to your husband's life and demanding that I give up my own interests in it. I refused. I am willing to change the way that I play my game in exchange for your… unlimited assistance… in dealing with Satan." The Frenchman leaned back in his chair and his voice once again took on a weary note. "I hate to call upon aid of any sort but to defeat this villain would take time that I do wish to spend."

"How about this?" Kelly countered. "You stop making threats to my husband and then we'll consider helping you. It sounds to me like you're still planning to act as judge, jury and executioner over Lazarus and that's not going to happen."

"I am proposing that we work together to defeat Doctor Satan, mademoiselle. In the course of that alliance I will observe your husband up close and decide based upon that if he is an innocent man. If you are confident that he is, then I give you my word that if I agree, I will seek to do no harm to him or any of his family."

"You still haven't told me what 'crimes' Lazarus has committed," Kelly replied icily. "Tell me that and then we'll talk about working together."

"Very well," he replied. "But I warn you: this shall not be an easy thing to hear. I assume that you're unaware that your husband has murdered the various members of Assistance Unlimited on multiple occasions?"

"What--?"

"I speak the truth, I assure you! And if my suspicions are true, your man is not all that he once was… and it may take a powerful catalyst to bring about the needed change to restore him."

———⊶⊶⊷———

THE LOCATION THAT Twitch had given to Assistance Unlimited was located in an unincorporated area located partway between Sovereign and Hancock, not far from L'Homme Fantastique's lair. It was the only house in a small cul-de-sac and was a two-story affair, painted such a dark shade of blue that it almost appeared black. The windows were all curtained, preventing Lazarus from looking within.

Lazarus approached the front steps, his eyes slowly moving from left to right. The yard was barren, with dead grass and a few uncared-for shrubs. Abby and Eun were close behind him and at a gesture, they split up, each moving around the rear of the house. Lazarus waited before the front door until they returned and informed him that there were no signs of life or of a trap waiting to be sprung.

Reaching for the door, Lazarus tried the knob and found that the door was unlocked. It swung open with a creak, revealing the darkened interior. All three of the heroes activated their flashlights and they entered slowly, casting the beams of light over dust-covered furniture and bare walls. There was a musty odor that implied that no one had been here in quite some time... which flew in the face of Twist's claims that he and Doctor Satan frequently met here.

"This is a trap," Eun hissed. He had shared this view multiple times on the drive over. Abby frowned at him and he replied with a shrug. "I still say we should have just torched the place - if Satan's here, he'll skedaddle out the front door and we'll catch him. If he's not, we remove an eyesore."

"Hush," Lazarus said and Eun fell silent. All three of them had entered the front room, which was decorated in a very old-fashioned style. Abby was reminded of her grandmother's home - even the scent was familiar, an old person's soap, a slightly medicinal odor designed to cover up the smell of urine that always lurked just below the surface.

A squeak came from upstairs and Lazarus immediately stopped in place, gesturing for the others to do the same. The sound repeated and Lazarus turned towards the stairs located in the foyer. He led the way up, drawing his pistol. Abby's lips moved silently, uttering a small spell that caused her hands to glow with blue energy. Eun brought up the rear, his hands clenched into fists.

At the top of the stairs Lazarus spotted an unusual room equipped with a solid metal door outside a regular wooden one, which could be slid shut if need be. Unlike the rest of the house, this room was illuminated -- a single lightbulb hung from the ceiling, swinging slightly. The chain squeaked every time the lightbulb moved to and fro. Lazarus noticed that the windows in this room were nailed shut and had a metal mesh over them - it reminded him of some of the asylums he had visited over the years, especially those designed to house dangerous patients. The only furnishings were a heavy metal chair resting against one of the walls and a cot fitted with dirty sheets.

Lazarus stepped into the room, followed by his companions. He reached up and seized hold of the light's chain, stopping its motion. His eyes scanned the mostly bare room, finally stopping on a metal grate at the base of one of the walls - it was part of the house's air circulation system and even though he didn't sense any air blowing out of the vent, it had to be -- how else would the light have been set in motion?

The wooden door suddenly slammed shut, followed a split second later by the clanging of the metal door.

"I hate to say I told you so," Eun muttered.

"Then don't," Abby said. She turned to the wooden door and expelled the blue energy that swirled around her hands. The barrier splintered easily but her eldritch blast did nothing more than darken the metal door. She paused her attack, concern twisting her features. "That's not ordinary steel, Lazarus. It's been tempered with spells to make it resistant to magical attacks."

Eun coughed and clutched at his chest. "Am I the only one having trouble breathing?"

Abby blinked, realizing that her own throat was starting to constrict. "No. I am, too."

Lazarus had already noticed the nature of this trap. Gas had been pumped into this room, which was what had caused the lightbulb to swing. Now, with the windows and doors barred, the members of Assistance Unlimited were unable to escape the effects of the invisible fumes.

"Eun!" Lazarus yelled. He didn't need to say any more. Eun and Abby each reached into pockets on their individual clothing and brought forth a handkerchief which they pressed tightly over their nostrils and mouth. Lazarus pulled out a handkerchief, as well, but he tied it as tightly as he could in bandit-bandana fashion. This left his hands free and he picked up the heavy steel chair, advancing towards the mesh-covered windows.

Gas of all types was a frequently-used weapon that the underworld employed against the members of Assistance Unlimited so the team was always prepared. Each of the men kept a coat lapel saturated with a chemical of Bob's invention that would nullify the effects of nearly any type of gas and, in addition, they all carried at least one handkerchief that was similarly saturated.

Lazarus drew the chair back and it whistled through the air before slamming against the metal shield like a steam hammer on a boiler plate. The mesh seemed completely unharmed and Eun turned away, figuring that his friend was taking on a hopeless battle. Instead, the young Korean-American began examining the metal door to see if there was any way it could be pried open. Abby, meanwhile, was trying to prepare a spell that would teleport them all free of the room but her mind was addled by the gas that she had already breathed in and the words of the spell were proving too slippery for her mind to seize hold of.

The metal chair slammed against the steel mesh twice more - and the chair was beginning to take on the shape of a pretzel. Lazarus wheezed from the exertion. He was unable to shield his nose and mouth from the gas the way his companions were but he saw, even if no one else did, that his efforts were beginning to have an effect: the mesh was starting to give a little in the center.

Eun turned and gaped. He had never before seen blows and he doubted that he'd ever see the like of them again. Lazarus was repeating the act of slamming the chair against the mesh and under the impact, the two metal chair legs were bent around on themselves. The mesh was now bellied inward in the middle like the bottom of a dishpan with a hundred-pound rock dropped on it from a third-story window.

One more blow and the mesh cracked open, leaving Lazarus to toss aside the ruined chair. He reached his hands in through the crack, between steel and window frame, and braced his feet against the wall. Using shoulders, legs, and arms, he pulled on the mesh... and after several seconds of seemingly no change in the situation, the protective barrier suddenly came off in the hero's hands. It had scarcely dropped to the floor before Lazarus was driving a fist through the glass of the window. The gas was pulled out of the room and Lazarus shoved his head out into the fresh air, taking several large gulps before squeezing his body through the opening. He reached back in with one hand and wheezed, "Come on! Quickly!"

The three of them were outside and climbing down the trellis within minutes. Lazarus had inhaled more of the gas than anyone else so his vision was still swimming and Eun was patting him on the back when Abby said, "Doctor Satan. He's here!"

Lazarus looked up to see the silhouette of Doctor Satan standing near their parked car. The horns atop the man's head looked especially sinister in the dim lighting.

"Well, well," Satan purred, "I wasn't expecting visitors tonight. I'm disappointed to see that you damaged my home. Are you going to pay for repairs?"

Eun's response was an animalistic roar accompanied by a sudden sprint that closed the distance between himself and Doctor Satan within seconds. Eun leaped into the air, tackling the villain and knocking him to the ground. The villain landed with a grunt but made no move to defend himself, not even when Eun began delivering one powerful blow after another. Satan's nose was shattered, sending blood spraying over his face, which quickly became just as scarlet the clothing he wore.

Abby looked at Lazarus and noted that he hadn't yet moved to pull Eun off their foe. She assumed that he was still staggered from the amount of gas she had inhaled so moved to do it herself - she grabbed Eun's arm as he drew it back for another blow.

"Stop! He's down!" she's shouted.

Eun shook his head. Satan was making a hacking sound and as the villain coughed out a wad of bloody phlegm it became clear that Satan was laughing. "No, he's not! Listen to him!"

Doctor Satan rolled onto his side, blood leaking into the earth. "You're dead and you just don't know it yet, Jiwon."

"What did you say?" Abby asked.

Satan twisted so he could look at Abby. "He's dead... my face is coated with a toxin that I discovered in the Philippines. There's no cure for it... the only reason it doesn't kill me is because I used a mixture of countermeasures and spells to protect me. Every time he hit me, he allowed more of it to seep through his flesh." Satan looked up at Eun and laughed once more.

An inarticulate grunt came from Eun's throat and his entire body suddenly seized up, the veins on his forehead standing out and blood dripping from his nose. He toppled off of Doctor Satan, his body beginning to flop about like a fish out of water. Abby gasped and fell to her knees beside him, calling upon a healing spell that she always kept close to her lips. Even as she laid hands upon him, a blue glow around her fingertips, she knew it was going to be in vain. Eun's eyes had rolled up into his skull and his lips were pulling back into a rictus grin.

Lazarus came forward and angrily gripped Satan by his cloak. He wrapped it tightly around the villain's face to prevent any accidentally touching. "If you've killed him," he hissed into Satan's ear, "I'll see to it that you're never free again."

Doctor Satan spoke loudly through the cloth. "What are you going to do, Lazarus? Let him really die this time? If you're going to bring him back from the dead, are you going to let Abby know how it works? Or do you have to kill her, too, to protect your secret?"

"What's he talking about?" Abby asked, tears beginning to form in her eyes as she cradled Eun's head in her lap. She wasn't worried about touching him - even if the toxin in his bloodstream could be passed on to another, she would risk it.

The only answer she received was in the form of a loud cracking sound - Lazarus had changed his grip on the cloak and given it a savage twist which resulted in the villain's neck snapping. Abby stared with wide eyes - it wasn't that she didn't wish Satan dead... he had, after all, just killed her friend... but Lazarus was usually so methodical in dealing with his enemies, even those that had brought great harm to him and his family.

"Lazarus...?" Abby asked as she lay Eun's head on the ground and began to rise. Her friend and mentor had tossed Satan's body aside like a bag of garbage and he was now approaching her. "What was Doctor Satan talking about?"

"Abigail. Stand where you are. I can explain." His right hand drifted towards the gun that he'd shoved into the waistband of his pants.

Something in the dead stare that Lazarus was giving her froze the blood in her veins. She threw up both hands, palms raised towards Lazarus, and before she'd even given thought to her actions she generated a pulse of energy that slammed into Lazarus and lifted him right off his feet. He flew back and landed right next to Satan's corpse.

Abby wasn't sure what was happening but she knew it was awful: Eun was dead, Lazarus had killed Doctor Satan, Satan had accused Lazarus of things that she didn't fully understand (raising the dead? killing her?), then Lazarus had started to draw a weapon on her.

Whatever all this meant, Abby wanted to get back to headquarters and find out the answers with the others. Even as Lazarus was getting to his knees, she readied another burst of energy that would send him into unconsciousness. Just before she could fire the blast, Lazarus muttered, "Majestros," and Abby felt her entire world turn upside down. Somewhere in her brain a switch had just been thrown and suddenly her magical power seemed to boil up from the pit of her being and overwhelm her. She screamed in pain as her heart began to pound and her eyes grew so hot that they swelled and burst. Even as her skin began to peel away from her bones, her heart burst, saving her from the agony that followed.

Lazarus struggled to his feet, exhaling slowly. Majestros was a kill-word that he'd implanted in her consciousness. She was a dangerous one and he'd known that eventually he might need to have a backup to take her down - for her own good, of course. She had been saved in the past by the same process that would now save both her and Eun once more. He hated to do this, it sickened him, but he was in too deep now… and, as he kept reminding himself, it wasn't like they were truly dying. They would come back, good as new, and remain his trusted, loyal friends. The city needed them… the world needed them… and he needed them, most of all.

Steeling himself, Lazarus began the process of dragging the remains of the dead to his car.

It would be a long drive home.

CHAPTER X
A WORLD OF TRUTH AND A WORLD OF LIES

SAMANTHA GRACE LEANED back in her chair, closing her eyes for a brief moment. Though she was only twenty-eight years old, she was beginning to realize that her youth was fading fast... she needed more sleep than before and there were little aches and pains that were now commonplace. Becoming a mother had only hastened the feeling that she was now and forevermore an Adult, with all the responsibilities that came with that word.

Born to wealthy parents, Samantha had grown up with every opportunity possible. She could speak five languages fluently, was a champion swimmer and was a veritable encyclopedia on topics as varied as fashion, European history and the socio-political climate of the Orient. Samantha had come into Gray's employ after her father had fallen prey to a blackmail scheme involving a half-sister that Samantha hadn't known about at the time. Lazarus had managed to apprehend the criminal behind the plot, managing to destroy the photographs that could have compromised her family's good name. Admiration for the work that Lazarus performed had led the then twenty-year-old into seeking a position with Assistance Unlimited, much to her father's chagrin. Eventually, she had come to regard the men and women of Assisted Unlimited as more than coworkers - they were friends and family. With them, she had conquered the few fears that had always haunted her and even come to forge a bond with her half-sister, Charity. She couldn't imagine life without Lazarus and the others.

"Miss Grace?"

Samantha sat up quickly. The door to the team's monitor room had been left open and Fitzgerald was standing there, looking a bit sheepish. "What is it?" she asked.

The young author stepped into the room and took a seat in one of the chairs against the wall. "I know that some of your adventures are fictionalized in the magazines…"

"Those pulps?" she replied, thinking of the cheap and often lurid story magazines that had hit their peak a few years before. They were produced quickly and as inexpensively as possible, unlike the so-called "slicks" that featured higher-brow work and paid a lot more to their contributors. "In the early days of our work, we sometimes struggled to pay the bills. It was Morgan's ideas to sell the rights to one of those publishers. Every month we let their editors look through some of our files -- we make sure that they aren't allowed to see anything that ought to remain private. They're free to extrapolate or embellish as they see fit."

"And… well, I was kind of hoping that since my current writing gig is kaput…"

"That we'd put in a good word for you with editors at Street & Smith?"

"Yes," Fitzgerald muttered, looking embarrassed.

Samantha leaned forward with her elbows on her knees. "I think you're really ignoring something big here."

"What's that?"

"You're sitting on a hell of a story here. Hired by a madman to write his memoirs before finding out that you're a tool in his scheme to destroy Assistance Unlimited--! You've got a bestseller right there and the best part is that you've already written a lot of it."

Fitzgerald rubbed his chin thoughtfully before a slow grin spread across his face. "I guess you're right! I didn't think of it that way." He chuckled and shook his head. "How do you do it, Miss Grace? Put up with all this craziness?"

"It's not always easy," she admitted. "But I just tell myself that all this weirdness would be happening whether I was here or not -- it's just if I weren't, I'd be like two-thirds of the world and not realize the truth about how bizarre life really is. Personally, I'm the kind of person that would rather know everything than live in some kind of lie."

"Even if the truth wasn't what you wanted to hear?"

"Especially then," Samantha replied. A brief chiming sound made her turn back towards the monitors.

"Something wrong?" Fitzgerald asked, a note of fear in his voice.

"No." She tapped one of the screens, which showed Morgan and The Black Terror entering the building through the parking lot entrance. A mostly-familiar group of men and women were following them: The Heroes, with the additions of El Demonio and a strange man in light blue tunic and darker blue pants. "It's just Morgan and the Terror coming back... and it looks like they not only found The Heroes but convinced them to come with."

Standing up, she asked Fitzgerald if he wanted to come with her to greet them. With a nod, the would-be author followed her down the hall.

———— ❦ ————

LAZARUS GRUNTED AS he dragged Eun's body up through the trapdoor hidden in the floor. He had built a secret tunnel under Robeson Avenue, allowing him to exit and enter his hidden lair without having to go through the rest of the building. It was an addition that he'd added after one person too many had spied his comings and goings through the study.

The corpse of his young friend was set beside the remains of Satan and Abby. He never disposed of the bodies outside the confines of his home - there was too much chance that something might be found by the authorities or by the newspapers... and then how would he explain the fact that one or more of his companions had died but were still running around?

No, it was best to use his acid vats to dissolve the bodies and then he would grind up the remaining bones and spread them about the property. Lazarus found the entire thing distasteful but he had convinced himself of its necessity. He walked over to the tanks containing the bodies of the 'new' Eun and Abby, touching the glass cases with affection. Soon they would be back, good as new.

Sudden pain shot through his head and he felt disoriented, much like he had at his birthday party. He reached out with one hand, feeling for a chair, and sank heavily into it. He saw a multiple of images in his mind: deaths and resurrections of his friends... but he also saw a place he'd hoped to put out of his mind for good.

He saw Carcosa, the land of dread. He saw the parched landscape, the dangerous animals, the strange lake that he had been forced to cross. Most strangely, he saw himself, looking ragged and tired, staring back at him, as if from across a vast distance.

Lazarus growled, shaking his head in an attempt to clear it of these images. It was impossible - he had escaped and he would never go back again... so why was he seeing it now?

The 'other' Lazarus - the one looking at him in an almost accusatory fashion - faded from view but Lazarus was left shaken by the visions. When he felt strong enough, he stood up and resumed his work... he needed to get rid of the bodies before he could unleash the resurrected ones.

He quickly lost himself in the process, grateful for the distraction from his hallucinations. Inside, his doubts had been pushed aside but not driven away. No matter how he might try to convince himself that what he was doing was for the good of his makeshift 'family,' the truth was that he knew it was wrong to keep the truth from them. Without truth, there could be no honor... and if one was dishonorable with those that loved you the most, what did that say about you as a person?

"THAT'S... INSANE."

Samantha turned away from Morgan and the others, one hand

raised to her mouth. She wasn't aware of the way she was trembling - her thoughts were racing, trying to wrap themselves around all that she had just been told.

At The Fighting Yank's urging, she had sent Fitzgerald back to his room… and then The Heroes had proceeded to lay out the full truth of their findings, with Morgan and Bob both corroborating their statements. As astounding as it all sounded, the worst part of it was that Samantha knew it as true. She couldn't exactly explain why - she didn't have any memories that suddenly returned to her mind nor did she have any physical evidence in front of her… but it *felt* like the truth.

The Golden Amazon placed a firm hand on her shoulder and Samantha found herself staring into the eyes of a woman that could easily pass for a goddess. "If it will put your doubts to rest, we should look at his lab. Morgan knows the entrance."

Samantha looked at Bob and then at Morgan. Both men nodded, looking just as haunted as she felt. "Lazarus hasn't come back yet - he's out with Abby and Eun. Should we call Kelly?"

"She'll need to know eventually," Bob said.

El Demonio shrugged his massive shoulders. "Let the senora hold on to her fantasies for a while longer… when her husband returns, we shall have to do things to him that would be hard for her to see."

Frowning, Samantha asked, "So what is the plan…? When we confront Lazarus, I mean."

"We'll cross that river when we come to it," The Fighting Yank said. "Of course we'll let him try to explain himself before we take any action."

Samantha considered it and reached for Morgan's hand. She held it tightly, letting him lead the way towards their friend's study. As the first two people recruited to join Assistance Unlimited, she and Morgan had always been especially close - when she'd first learned of her pregnancy, he'd volunteered his services as a husband. It had been a sweet gesture, reminding Samantha of the way that Morgan had carried a torch for her for many years. Their friendship survived her admission that she saw him as a father figure and not a lover, which gave ample evidence of how strong their bond really was.

She could only hope that the relationships she shared with the rest of Assistance Unlimited would be able to survive what came next.

EL DEMONIO STRODE through the halls of his enemies, feeling strangely unsatisfied. At first, it had amused him to know that Assistance Unlimited was being torn apart by internal strife... he saw it as a weakening of them and he hoped to take some credit for their inevitable demise.

Now, however, he found himself nervously flexing his muscles and frowning beneath his luchadore-style mask. He enjoyed defeating foes that were nearly as powerful as he, using his skills, intellect and strength to vanquish them. Fighting them while they were wounded took away some of the challenge and left him feeling empty. The more he saw these 'heroes,' the more he realized how wounded they truly were... Lazarus Gray had brought them together, he had inspired them, and he had kept them working in unison through the force of his will. Finding out that he had betrayed them and had feet of clay had cast them into disarray... destroying them now would almost not be worth the effort.

He caught the one called Blue Fire staring at him and he asked, "You have a problem with me, muchacho?"

"Not really," Blue Fire replied. "I mean, I don't trust you - the others have told me enough about you that I wouldn't do that - but I was just wondering if you felt as out of place as I do. It's a really personal deal for the rest of them but I've never met Lazarus. I only know him through stories."

"I know what you mean, muchacho... It almost feels like we are intruding in some private family matter."

"That's it exactly!" Blue Fire said with a smile. Despite his claim to not trust El Demonio, the crime lord felt sure that the American liked him. He had that effect on many people -- they were drawn to him like moths to a flame. That was how he had risen through the ranks of the criminal world so quickly -- that and his penchant for murder. "If trouble breaks out," Blue Fire continues, "you and I can make a good team. Nobody can hurt me when I activate my powers so it makes sense for me to rush in first... while Lazarus or whomever is wasting time trying to hit me, you can sneak in and punch them out. We'll be a real dynamic duo like those guys in the comics... Batman and Robin!"

El Demonio reached out and grabbed Blue Fire's arm. "Keep your mind on el trabajo, amigo. This is a job, not a game. And you were right before - you should not trust me." He released his grip on the youth, feeling a mixture of shame and power when he saw the sudden rush of fear in the gringo's eyes.

When they reached the study, Morgan walked straight towards a particular book on the crowded shelves - an oversized copy of the Bible bound in leather, jutting just a bit farther off the shelf than it should have. He paused before touching it, casting a lingering glance around the room. There was no way he could even count the number of times he had been here, sometimes with Lazarus, sometimes without... but he knew that this time would alter his life forever. There would be no turning back - even if Lazarus killed them all and brought them back, The Heroes had set certain things in motion that would reveal all if they were not stopped before a particular hour.

"Morgan...?" Samantha whispered. "Are you okay?"

Morgan didn't know whether to laugh or cry. Instead, he shook his head and replied, "No, Sam, I'm not okay. I don't know if I'll ever be okay again. When I met Lazarus, I was a criminal. He showed me that I could be something better, he made me believe in myself in a way that I never thought I could. And now... now he's a damned murderer!"

"No, he's not." Samantha said it with such ferocity that it brought Morgan up short. "Something's wrong with him. Something bad. And whatever it is, we'll figure it out and we'll help him... because he deserves that. He's helped all of us too many times to count -- and he wasn't always a murderer. You know that. I know that. And even the rest of these 'Heroes' would know that if they just stopped long enough to think about it. *He is not - and never will be - a bad guy.* He's our friend.

He's our inspiration. And right now he needs us to fix whatever's wrong with him. Okay?"

Morgan smiled just a little. "Okay, Sam. You convinced me."

A twist of the book and the wall slid open, revealing Lazarus' sanctum for all to see.

CHAPTER XI
TOWER OF BABEL

"OH, MY GOD," gasped Olga as she entered the laboratory. It wasn't the nude bodies of her friends floating in their tanks that elicited the call to a higher power -- it was the large circular tub in the back of the room that produced an awful stench... and from which body parts were protruding, slowly being dissolved in acid.

Being possessed of a firmer constitution than most, The Golden Amazon approached the container and covered her nose to avoid inhaling the fumes directly. Something bobbed up out of the acid at that moment, revealing the partially burned features of Eun Jiwon. The Amazon grimaced, particularly when part of a female breast floated by Eun's face. "It's Abby and Eun," she said aloud.

Samantha turned away, her eyes suddenly brimming with tears. Despite her words of just a moment before, she was suddenly filled with doubt. How could Lazarus do this...? Even if he were sick or possessed or whatever it was, surely the strongest part of himself would have rebelled?

Her vision was still obscured by tears when pandemonium broke out all around her. She heard Olga cry out and suddenly fall past Samantha's line of sight, clutching at her face. Some sort of silvery powder was all over Olga's eyes and nose and Olga was screaming as she wiped at her face in a futile attempt to brush it off.

Spinning about and wiping her eyes with the back of her hand, Samantha saw Lazarus in the room. He was spinning and whirling like a dervish, a knife in one hand and a mystic artifact in the other - Samantha recognized it as The Gem of G'vos, a fist-sized stone the color of dried blood. She wasn't quite sure what properties it possessed - it was, after all, only one of hundreds of strange objects that Assistance Unlimited had recovered over the years. Her memory was jogged when she saw Lazarus duck below a punch thrown by The Black Terror and Lazarus jammed the Gem up against Bob's midsection. Immediately the leather-clad hero was engulfed in a strange golden flame that sent him to the floor, his entire form completely paralyzed.

Samantha took a few steps back as Lazarus sprang up onto a nearby counter, knocking off a set of glass beakers that shattered on the floor. He delivered a kick right into Morgan's face, sending the older man staggering back, before throwing his knife with unerring accuracy - it caught El Demonio in the side of the throat, just missing being a killing blow. The masked villain roared in anger and started towards Lazarus but he suddenly began staggering before slipping to his knees. His eyes bulged beneath the mask and he yanked the knife from his throat,, realizing that its edge was tinged with some sort of fast-acting poison.

Leaping off the counter, Lazarus landed on the shoulders of The Golden Amazon, positioned as if they were about to play a game of chicken fight in a pool or stream. She didn't try to dislodge him - rather she slammed her body towards the wall, crushing Lazarus between the hard surface and her own super-dense body. Lazarus grunted but the fight went out of the Amazon when the Gem was slammed hard against the side of her head, resulting in her falling prey to the same paralysis that had affected The Black Terror.

At this point, The Fighting Yank had obviously seen enough. "Lazarus! Stop this! We'll give you the chance to explain!" He reached out and grabbed hold of Lazarus' arm, squeezing hard enough that the founder of Assistance Unlimited grunted in pain and he lost his grip on the Gem. It fell to the floor with a clatter but Lazarus was far from finished.

Even while the Yank still held one of his arms, Lazarus was stretching his body so that his other hand could make contact with a metal rod that lay on a nearby table. What its purpose was, Samantha had no clue, but she saw it put to ready use now: decades of single-stick battle practice guided her friend's four-second blur of six blows: two lateral swings to break the Yank's right arm; two vertical swings to the underside of the Sentinel of Liberty's jaw, dropping him to his knees; and two fluidly vicious downward swings - both of which would have crushed the skull of a normal man but which left the Fighting Yank in a state of semi-consciousness.

Lazarus stepped away, breathing heavily. The metal rod was now held at his side, a bit of blood dripping from its tip. Slowly he turned his gaze towards the only two people that remained upright aside from himself: Samantha and the young man known as Blue Fire.

Deliberately, Lazarus knelt down and picked up the Gem. He held it up towards Blue Fire and said, "This can affect you even when you go intangible." Seeing surprise in the younger man's eyes, Lazarus added, "I make it my business to keep up with unusual people such as yourself."

Jack paused only a brief moment before he clenched his fists and resolutely said, "I'm sorry, Mr. Gray, but I'm afraid I can't take your word for that. What you're doing here is wrong -- and I'm ashamed to say that I've always looked up to you as an example of what a hero should be." Blue Fire suddenly ignited, his unusual-colored flames racing up and down his body. He lunged forward, intending to pass through Lazarus - such a maneuver usually disoriented his foes and allowed him to solidify behind them. It was usually a quick action to then knock them out before they could figure out what he had done.

Unfortunately, Lazarus was being truthful in his warning. As soon as Blue Fire began to pass through the other man's body, the Gem sent intense pain through his otherwise intangible form. Screaming in shock, Blue Fire pulled back and almost instantly noticed that he was unable to move in any way. He fell over, solid once more. The strange paralysis that had affected the other victims of the Gem had claimed one more victim.

"Samantha," Lazarus said, shifting his attention away from Blue Fire. He looked at her with an expression that touched her heart, despite all that she had seen and heard. He looked almost haunted as he whispered, "I'm sorry."

"For what? The lies? Or the fact that you're about to kill me?" Samantha tried to sound angry but her voice quavered -- it was more from hurt and disappointment than from fear.

Lazarus shook his head and what he said next almost sounded more like he was trying to convince himself more than he was Samantha. "It's not murder... not really. You'll be back, same as before. Maybe even better. Haven't you noticed how many times you and the others have been shot or stabbed? Normal people don't shrug that off... but you do. Your body isn't covered with scars, not like mine is."

"That doesn't make it okay, Lazarus... What made you like this? Has Doctor Satan been controlling you? Or is it something else? Tell me and I'll help you. It's not too late." Samantha dropped into a fighting stance when Lazarus took a step towards her. "I won't go down easy, Lazarus. I promise you that."

Lazarus's face, which had remained impassive during all of this, now showed a flicker of regret. "I know you won't. You never do."

"**S**AMANTHA - DUCK!"

Samantha dropped into a crouch as soon as she heard Kelly's voice from behind her. She didn't know what was about to happen but she saw no reason not to trust that Kelly was on her side - what was the alternative, after all? Looking over her shoulder, she saw Kelly standing in the doorway with a purple-garbed man that she knew must be the famous L'Homme Fantastique -- and this man was armed with a strange-looking firearm that had an oversized barrel and the oddest loading cartridge that she'd ever laid eyes upon.

The gun discharged and a dart-like object flew towards Lazarus. For a split second Samantha feared that her friend would somehow dodge the blast - she'd seen him do similar feats of agility before. He held his ground, however, not even taking a step to the left or right. It was almost as if he was ready for someone to stop him.

The dart struck him in the throat, just below his Adam's apple, and its effect was instantaneous. Lazarus began to sway, letting his weapons fall to the floor, and he tried and failed to reach out and grab hold of a nearby counter to stop his own descent. Lazarus fell forward and it was Kelly that rushed forward to catch him in her arms. She lowered him gently to the floor before looking around at Samantha with wide eyes.

"Sam?" Kelly asked.

"Yes?"

"Call Doctor Hancock and get him down here on the double. Some of our friends need immediate care."

Nodding in understanding, Samantha rushed out of the lab and back into the study, where she plucked up a phone from the desk. She hurriedly dialed the phone number for the group's 24/7 on-call physician.

Kelly, meanwhile, looked at L'Homme Fantastique and said, "That man in England that you told me about on the way over here..."

"Yes, mademoiselle?" the mysterious figure replied. He seemed to be floating around the room, occasionally stopping to check on one of the fallen heroes.

Kelly's voice was commanding. "Get him here... now."

NATHANIEL CAINE RAN a hand through his longish brown hair and sat down in the battered leather chair that he'd used for the entire tenure of his career with the London police. It creaked and sagged but he loved it - it had molded itself to the curvature of his body just perfectly and as far as he was concerned, it was the best chair in the building. Twice there had been attempts to have his chair retired to the trash bin and a new one installed in its place but Nat had caught wind of both attempts and made sure that they weren't successful.

With a sigh, he started looking through reports that littered his desk, signing off on forms here and there. To most people's eyes, Nat looked like a reasonably attractive man but there was nothing particularly memorable about him... only a select few knew that he was one of the Gifted, a subset of humanity able to manipulate magical energy. In fact, he was The Catalyst, the high mage of the 20th century. He knew that there had been many Catalysts before him but he'd never learned who they were or what lives they had led[8]... perhaps someday he'd uncover those sorts of details but for now it was all a mystery to him.

It wasn't that long ago that he'd discovered his abilities, found the love of his life, and aided the masked American vigilante known as The Peregrine in stopping a Nazi plot to create their own alternate Earth[9]. Since then he'd split his time between police work and delving into the supernatural subculture in London. It turned out that there was a thriving black market in mystical goods and plenty of people willing to sell their bodies, their time, and even their souls to get access to them. As such, Nat felt like he never really had any time off - when he wasn't dealing with run-of-the-mill criminals, he and Rachel were investigating illegal Fairy Dust operations, centaur pornography rings, and other bizarre forms of crime.

The phone perched on the corner of the paper-laden desk suddenly vibrated, just as it always did when it rang. Nat automatically reached for it but his fingers paused just short of picking up the receiver. He hadn't fully noticed it but something was off... had the phone rang at all? Suddenly the phone once more vibrated - but once again, there was no sound accompanying the activity. A moment of confusion made Nat glance around at the rest of the floor - a handful of officers were busy in their own affairs, whether that was talking in low tones with each other or working on paperwork like Nat had been doing.

Frowning, Nat picked up the receiver and asked, "Hello?"

The voice on the other line spoke English with a strong French accent. "Mon ami, my apologies for having bothered you at work but this is something that cannot be delayed. I am contacting you because of your... ah, how do you say it?... your 'moonlighting' job?"

"Who is this?" Nat asked, keeping his voice down so as to not attract any attention from his peers. He was sitting straight now, his heart beginning to hammer in his chest. He'd tried very hard to keep

---

8   Andre Thierry appeared in several volumes of Lazarus Gray as well as in the crossover novel Gotterdammerung - he was Nathaniel's predecessor as Catalyst.

9   A story reprinted in The Peregrine Omnibus Volume One.

his supernatural affairs out of the office... so who had figured out the connection?

"I go by the rather dramatic name of L'Homme Fantastique... and I am currently at 6196 Robeson Avenue in Sovereign City. Are you familiar with the address?"

"...Yes. I've heard of it before." Nat's mind was suddenly filled with images from newsreels and lurid magazine covers: Lazarus Gray and his plucky band of Assistance Unlimited allies, battling one amazing menace after another. "You're calling me all the way from the United States?"

"It's magic," L'Homme Fantastique replied with the barest hint of a chuckle. "Now, would you be so kind as to excuse yourself from the office and come join us? It is a matter of grave import."

Nathaniel stood, still holding the receiver against his ear. "Can you give me a bloody clue what this is about?"

There was no trace of humor in the words that came in reply to that question. In fact, the way they were stated froze the blood in Nathaniel's veins. "It concerns Lazarus Gray's eternal soul," L'Homme Fantastique said - and then the line went dead.

<hr />

TY BARRON, THE diminutive killer dubbed Little Lord Murderboy, ignored the terrified moans of the big-breasted blonde that was tied spread-eagled on the cold tile floor. She lay in the center of a crudely drawn pentagram, completely naked, a gag tied around her mouth.. Murderboy would have ordinarily enjoyed seeing the goosebumps rising up on her flesh and the way her heavy breasts jiggled as she shivered in fear but he had far more important things on his mind at the moment.

The girl was Chester's secretary, who had tried to flee at the sound of her boss being liquidated. Murderboy had known she could be useful to him so he'd had her rounded up, stripped, and thrown into the back of his car, where she'd ridden in wide-eyed horror alongside Murderboy, who had spent the entire trip reading through the strange book he'd received.

Much of the tome had been a confusing mess of ideas that Barron couldn't understand... but there were references to a place called Carcosa and a powerful entity known as The King in Yellow. From what Murderboy could gather, this 'King' would sometimes bestow incredible power on human beings in exchange for their soul... given that Murderboy didn't believe in such crazy notions as a soul in the first place, he had little reason to not bargain it away if someone would give him something in return for some mystical nonsense like his soul.

According to the book, it was possible to open a portal to this Carcosa place with the sacrifice of a pure-hearted person... and Murderboy wasn't sure if this dame fit that description but he was willing to find out.

"Hey, boss, we got the knife."

Murderboy looked over to see that two of his minions - beefy guys with shit for brains named Maurice and Tony - had entered the room. It was Tony that had spoken and he was holding a large knife in one hand. Its blade gleamed in the room's light and caused the girl to begin crying even worse. Maurice was staring at her like a lion studying a wounded gazelle.

"Hand it here, you moron." Murderboy grabbed the knife and walked over to the sobbing girl. He stood with one foot on either side of her well-endowed chest and tilted his head to the side. "Stifle it, sister. All that crying ain't gonna save your life, okay?"

These words had the opposite effect from what he intended as the naked woman began crying all the harder, even trying to beg for mercy around the gag. Murderboy reached up and rubbed the spot in-between his eyes where his headaches always seemed to form. A moment later, he rolled his neck, causing it to pop loudly and then he raised the knife over his head and brought it down hard. He repeated the action again and again, stabbing through skin and bone, leaving her lovely bosom a bloody mess that was no longer worthy of a lingering male gaze.

All the while that he had been hacking away, ending the poor girl's life, he had been muttering under his breath, hoping that he was pronouncing the words right. They were crazy and he wasn't convinced they were English but what did he know? He just had to hope that intent carried as much weight as accuracy.

When it was done, he straightened, breathing heavily, his knife dripping with gore. He looked around, fully prepared to be disappointed. Truth be told, he thought most 'magic' was nothing but a bunch of lies and trickery... but he'd figured it was worth taking a chance.

He gasped, however, upon seeing that Maurice and Tony were not there... Neither, in fact, was the room in which he'd murdered the girl. Likewise, her corpse was gone... Murderboy was standing on an alien landscape with cracked earth beneath his feet. As he slowly turned, taking in his surroundings, he saw a darkened sky with a bloated blood-red moon that seemed far too close to the surface... and across the face of this moon flew a creature that resembled a pterodactyl -- if said pterodactyl had six legs and a crown of fire that hovered round its reptilian head.

"Goddamn," he muttered. "It worked."

CHAPTER XII
TWILIGHT

THE FOLLOWING TWENTY-FOUR hours were tense ones. The Black Terror had released the new versions of Eun and Abby from their tanks and both had been told of Lazarus's crimes. The Catalyst had arrived from England and found himself not only intrigued by the idea of finding out what was wrong with the famous Lazarus Gray but also by the fact that many of these men and women were familiar with his predecessor.

Lazarus himself was locked away in the prison that he had helped create. Tartarus was now home to its master and he was bound hand and foot, as well as having a metal band fastened about his neck. There would be no taking chances with him - especially in light of the way he had nearly defeated the entire membership of both Assistance Unlimited and The Heroes single-handedly.

Nathaniel, clad in the skintight emerald uniform that marked him as The Catalyst, stood at the rear of the team's meeting room, watching as men and women that he knew only from newspaper accounts and newsreel footage spoke in hushed tones. He felt wildly out of place but when he spotted Kelly Gray and the purple-garbed L'Homme Fantastique step aside from the rest of the group, his police detective instincts took over and he subtly moved closer to them, pretending not to listen to their conversation.

"Satan's dead," Kelly murmured. "So why are you still here...? You don't need our help anymore."

L'Homme Fantastique chuckled, his face somehow hidden in

shadow beneath the wide brim of his hat - no matter how he turned to the light, that same shadow always seemed to hide his features. "I am not certain that our mutual enemy is truly dead - his history is rife with instances where he was seemingly killed, only to reappear at a later date."

"His body was dissolved in acid," Kelly pointed out. "I don't think he'll be reappearing from that."

"We shall see, mademoiselle, we shall see." L'Homme Fantastique paused before adding, "Then, there is still the matter of judging your husband. To be fair, at this point there is little doubt as to his guilt. I have only refrained from punishing him because it seems that your friends are going to do that for me."

"My husband isn't evil."

"You don't sound too certain of that."

"Then you aren't listening clearly." Kelly spun about and walked to the center of the room. She raised her voice the same way her husband usually did, commanding the attention of everyone immediately. "We've waited long enough, I think. It's time, Mr. Caine. Are you ready to begin?"

Catalyst stepped forward and cleared his throat. As a police officer, he was used to public speaking and being in control - but now his heart beat wildly in his chest and he had to hope that his voice didn't betray him. He still felt like he was playing dress-up and pretending to be a hero -- these people were the real thing. "I worked a spell on Mr. Gray and, with some assistance from Miss Cross, I think I've been able to make sense out of what I saw. I believe that the man currently held at Tartarus is not actually Lazarus Gray… or at least, not all of him."

"What the hell does that mean…?" Morgan asked.

The Fighting Yank placed a gloved hand on the other man's shoulder. "Patience," he cautioned.

Catalyst continued as if Morgan hadn't interrupted him. "From the things Abby told me, Lazarus spent some time in a cursed realm known as Carcosa a few years ago. Carcosa is one of the 12 Mirrored Realms

- a series of other realities that are connected to ours. The residents of those realms sometimes refer to our own by the somewhat derisive name of 'The Pale Reflection.' One of the unusual things about the Mirrored Realms is that sometimes people leave a piece of themselves behind... this is especially true if they come into contact with the patron entity of that realm -- in the case of Carcosa that entity is The King in Yellow."

"Lazarus defeated him," Kelly said. She was unconsciously twisting the collar of her blouse, squeezing it in an attempt to calm her nerves. "Of course, it seems like the evil things are never really beaten, are they? They just keep coming back, over and over again."

No one felt like that arguing that point. Assistance Unlimited had battled some of their foes - like the Egyptian sorceress named Femi - a half dozen times or more, often with the conflict ending with the apparent 'permanent' demise of their enemy.

Catalyst looked at Kelly with pity in his gaze. "A part of your husband was split from the whole and remains there. The longer his soul is cleaved in two, the more he drifts from his true nature. Something may begin as an idea that would normally be cast aside but now it takes root and without his full resolve, he gives in to behaviors that normally would be resisted. Sometimes this manifests as sexual deviancy or unusual emotional displays... or, in this case, a desire to protect the lives of his loved ones is taken to bizarre extremes."

Samantha could barely restrain the excitement she felt. With an unsteady smile and a glance around the room, she asked, "So what happened wasn't really his fault...?"

"I wouldn't go that far," Abby said, her eyes showing clear signs of having recently cried. "Lazarus did this... a *part* of him did this. Whatever happens next, whether or not we can 'fix' him... we can't forget that. We might forgive but we shouldn't forget."

Several in the room nodded or murmured a quiet assent and Catalyst waited until they were done before he forged ahead. "Abby asked something about 'what happens next' - well, what happens next is mostly up to Lazarus himself. We need to send him back to Carcosa where he needs to find his missing part of his soul... and once they're reunited, he can come home."

El Demonio spoke up. "There was a time when I had a storehouse of occult tomes... in one of them there was a collection of spells related to contacting the King in Yellow and accessing Carcosa. I remember one of the rituals involved the death of an innocent and the recitation of certain words."

"There's been enough death already," Morgan said. "We need another way."

"If you lack the guts to do it yourself, let me know," Demonio replied with a gruff laugh. He had one hand on the bandage taped to his neck. "Or maybe you just don't love your leader enough to do something that's distasteful, eh?"

Morgan started to take a step towards the masked man but Eun held him back, eliciting another chuckle from the villain.

Catalyst cleared his throat. "Abby and I can open a doorway to Carcosa... but someone needs to speak to Lazarus and convince him to find his missing soul and return. The doorway we open will close after a certain amount of time and if he hasn't merged with his other self, I'm not sure we'll get a second chance at this."

"I'll talk to him," Kelly said. "Give me an hour, can you?"

Abby nodded. "We can do that."

Morgan muttered testily, "And if you can't gently convince him, tell him that his ass will stay in this prison for the rest of his life if he doesn't go along with it!"

Kelly merely gave a nod as she exited the room. She knew that everyone was hurting right now but Lazarus was her husband and the father of her son... she had more to lose than anyone.

TARTARUS HAD BEEN built to house beings for whom normal prisons would not be enough. Whether it was due to enhanced intelligence, magical aptitude or some other enhanced ability, those that were incarcerated here found themselves in cells that were constantly monitored and their abilities were often nullified by special restraints.

Lazarus Gray had designed this prison, never suspecting that one day he would find himself locked away within its walls. He sat in a cell, his arms restrained by the sort of restraint jacket used in asylums. A magical barrier had been erected around the cell's door, preventing him from exiting the room even if he had managed to escape the straitjacket and the heavy chain wrapped around his left leg that was fastened to the wall.

The worst part of it all? Lazarus knew that he deserved this. Despite his desire to protect his friends, he had deceived them on a level that went beyond simple lying. He had not only kept from them the knowledge that they had died and been reborn multiple times... he had actually murdered them to protect his secret.

He recognized the footsteps long before his wife came into view, standing just outside the crackling eldritch barrier. She wore his favorite dress, a pair of stockings, and matching shoes. If it wasn't for the look of emotional agony written on her features, he might have thought she was dressed for a night on the town.

"Kelly, I'm glad you came." His voice sounded raspy - he needed to take a drink but no one had brought his meal yet. "I was worried you wouldn't want to see me."

"Don't be silly - of course I'd want to see you. We think we know what's wrong with you, Lazarus... and it's something that can be repaired but you have to be the one to do it."

"What do you mean?" Lazarus tried to rise but the chain on his leg and his inability to use his arms for balance prevented him from doing more than getting to his knees.

Kelly relayed what Catalyst and Abby had told her, being careful to emphasize that her husband's actions were the result of him being split in two. She was afraid that if he felt too guilty, he might think that there was nothing that could set things right again. When she was finished, Lazarus was still steadily looking at her. He hadn't made a sound or shifted his expression during her spiel.

When he finally spoke, Kelly felt her heart sink. Her fears seemed to be confirmed. He sounded like a beaten man. "Even if I managed to find the splintered part of my soul and was able to merge with it again, what will it change? No one will ever be able to look at me the same way again -- and even if they could, I'm not sure that I'll be able to stare them in the eyes and ask them to trust me. I've betrayed them. I've betrayed *you*."

"You've never given up on anything, Lazarus." Kelly stepped as close to the mystical gate as possible, standing so close to it that the ends of her hair lifted upward as the field exerted an electromagnetic effect on her body. "When your parents died, you threw yourself into your studies. When Walther Lunt invited you to join the Illuminati and you found out that they were evil, you dedicated yourself to exposing them. When they left you amnesiac on the shores of Sovereign City, you created a new life for yourself. Again and again you've faced madmen, demons, and Nazis. You *died*, Lazarus! And you fought your way back to us! What you've done is awful, yes... but we love you. All of us do! You've made all of us better just by being with us! Will it be easy to move forward after this? No. But we're all willing to try. And if we're willing, why the hell aren't you? Is this how you want it to end - with you locked up like an animal? With your friends broken and shattered? With your son growing up wondering what happened to his father?"

Lazarus lowered his eyes but Kelly could tell she was getting through to him: the set of his jaw, the way his breathing slightly quickened, the way his lips turned slightly downward at the edges. These almost imperceptible signs would have been invisible to nearly anyone else but Kelly knew her husband intimately and she was able to spot all the signs.

"So, what's it going to be, Lazarus? Are you going to rise up one more time and live up to your name?" she pressed.

Slowly, her husband managed to rise to his feet this time. It was unsteady given how he was confined but he was still somehow able to give the action an air of grace. With a determined voice, he asked, "What do I have to do?"

"Nothing much," she answered with a soft smile. "Just return to

Carcosa, locate your missing self, and somehow get him to merge with you... then make back before the portal we'll be opening closes and traps you there."

"Easy peasy," he replied. Given how emotionless his tone was, Kelly couldn't help but laugh at his choice of words. She reached up and wiped away a tear.

"Lazarus?"

"Yes?"

"I'm willing to forgive you. We all are. But if this isn't the end of it," she let an edge creep into her voice and Lazarus was reminded of the fiery spirit that had led him to fall in love with her. "I'll kill you myself before I let you harm our son. Do you understand?"

"I wouldn't expect anything less."

"He hasn't... he hasn't died, has he? You haven't--?"

"No. Never." Lazarus looked into his wife's eyes and she felt certain that he was being truthful... but given all the lies, how could she ever really know?

Kelly took a step back and nodded. "Let him loose," she said and it was then that Lazarus realized that she wasn't alone - someone had been standing off to the side, just out of his sight.

When the mystical field fell, Eun and Abby moved quickly into the cell. Neither of them looked him in the face and he knew that they were still warring with the knowledge that he'd recently re-grown both of them in tanks.

"I'll make this right," he said to Eun as the young man undid the leg restraint.

Eun glanced at him for the first time and nodded. "I believe you. If I didn't, I wouldn't be here."

Lazarus clasped his friend on the arm and then turned towards Abby but she was already exiting the cell - and he realized that some people's forgiveness would not be won as quickly.

LITTLE LORD MURDERBOY gasped as he straddled his foe, a leathery-skinned monster with one eye, a circular mouth lined with razor-sharp teeth, and claw-like hands. The crime boss held a bloody rock in his left hand, the stone spattered with bits of grey matter.

The creature had leaped upon the dwarf as he made his way through the barren landscape - it had hidden behind several boulders, flattening its thin body against the ground in order to evade detection.

Murderboy would have died if he hadn't managed to grab hold of a nearby rock while the monster strove to tear out his throat. The first blow that the dwarf had landed had almost been by chance but once he'd seized the initiative, Murderboy had let out a roar of triumph and proceeded to beat the creature until its head was a mess.

With a grimace, Murderboy stood up and backed away from the monster. He became aware that there were other eyes upon him - more of the creature's pack were lurking in the growing shadows as day transitioned into the spectral time of twilight but none of them seemed eager to engage him in battle, not when one of their fellows lay in a heap at his feet. He wondered why they didn't attack en masse and seek to overwhelm him but he assumed that they were mostly scavengers and shared the cowardly nature associated with those that favored eating the dead. Given the way the ribs of his fallen foe protruded against its flesh, he had to assume that this one had been pushed into attacking by starvation.

Murderboy checked and made sure that he still had his knife and pistol. Both remained attached to his belt but he suddenly wished that he had brought more ammunition with him… he would have to conserve his bullets.

A low groan reached his ears and he spun about, drawing his gun. All thoughts about saving his ammunition faded as he saw a horrific figure shambling in his direction. It was a skeletal figure wearing the tatters of a robe the color of aged straw. A crown forged of briars, twigs and human fingers lay atop the skull's brow. An odor of putrefaction drifted from the figure, assaulting Murderboy's nostrils and making him retch.

"Ty Barron," the figure said, its mouth opening and closing with little 'clacking' sounds. He saw no tongue in this awful maw so he did not know how it was able to talk - the sheer unreality of it made him feel that his sanity hung by a tenuous thread. "Why did you come?" it said, coming to a halt no more than four feet from him. It was a giant, standing well over eight feet in height - given his own short stature, it made the sense of power between them great indeed.

"Are you... the King in Yellow?" Murderboy stammered.

The figure waved one bony arm, taking in all that surrounded them. "I am what remains. I am the one that rules in the dark. I feed off the screams of the dying and the feverish moans of the sinful. You walk the pathways of my bowels and feed off the scabs of my flesh."

"So... is that a yes, then?" Murderboy answered. He hated all this mystical nonsense and his distaste for it crept into his words.

Murderboy was shocked by the rapidity of what happened next. The King in Yellow seized him by the throat and easily lifted the dwarf off his feet. Murderboy was brought close to the figure's skull, the stench causing his eyes to water.

"This 'humor' that humans possess, it has always confused me," the King in Yellow said. From deep in its eye sockets, tiny bursts of color could be seen... as if deep within, there was a fire burning, one that had come close to being snuffed out. "It is a sign of your people's immaturity. If you truly knew what lurked at the heart of the cosmos, if you had any conception of the ultimate lie that permeates all reality... you would not laugh. You would cry out and scurry into the darkness in the hopes that none of the higher powers might see you."

The King tossed Murderboy to the ground and the criminal grunted in pain. Twilight was fading fast, to be replaced by a terrible darkness... or perhaps the long shadows came from the King himself, Murderboy mused.

"I came because I want power," the dwarf said, slowly getting to his knees. He rubbed his right arm with his left hand - it hurt badly and he thought that he might have broken it. "You're supposed to have plenty of it... and I want some. Supposedly you want souls, right? Well, I ain't usin' mine."

The King in Yellow regarded him for a moment before leaning over him. "Poor, insignificant bug. I should squash you for having the temerity to waste my time."

Murderboy felt as if he'd been struck... something in that awful thing's gaze, in the way that the King in Yellow had dismissed him as a 'bug' suddenly seemed to validate all the doubts he'd always carried in his heart. That he was nothing... less than nothing.

"My enemy comes at last," the King said, and Murderboy suddenly felt a surge of hope. The towering figure looked around, as if afraid that his nameless foe might leap from the shadows at any moment. He finally returned his frightful gaze on the dwarf, saying, "He comes to collect that which he left behind. Destroy them both for me... and you shall have the power you seek. Fail... and your spirit will reside here in Carcosa for all eternity."

"Who's this enemy of yours?" Murderboy asked. This was something he could understand and deal with. The big guy had somebody he wanted whacked... if Murderboy did him a solid, he'd be willing to do one in return. That was how gangsters did it all the time.

The light in the King's eye sockets flared even brighter. "I sense his name is known to you. Kill Lazarus Gray for me - both of him!"

CHAPTER XIII
TO LIVE AND DIE IN CARCOSA

NIGHT CLUNG TO the cracked landscape like a heavy blanket. The moon that hung in the sky seemed to have lost its luster long ago - it only provided the barest illumination now, just enough to provide the man below with the light needed to finish stripping the carcass of its hide.

He had killed it with his bare hands, wrapping his strong, well-tanned fingers about its neck before flexing his muscles and giving its head a twist. When he'd first come here, it had been difficult to kill beasts like this, even in self-defense. He had become somewhat at ease with the violence over time but out of respect for those animals that he had to sacrifice, he made sure to use as much of the creature as possible so that nothing went to waste.

An unusual noise registered on his acute hearing and the man snapped to attention. It was the sound of footsteps outside his home -- and he had never heard such on this side of the lake. Grabbing hold of a homemade knife, he slowly moved to the window and looked out. He had erected torches to illuminate the path leading to his door and on this occasion they actually did their intended purpose: he saw a diminutive man dressed like a character from a book, one that he had read before he'd become trapped in Carcosa: Little Lord Fauntleroy. The oddity of the situation didn't give the man any pause -- this was a land of strangeness, after all. Just because he had never seen this individual before didn't mean that he was new - in all his travels, the man had never come close to mapping the borders of Carcosa and he wasn't certain that anyone ever could. This dimension, he had to come to believe, bordered on the realm of nightmare.

The funnily-garbed man began knocking at the front entrance but he must have sensed that he was being observed because he stepped away from the door and looked upward. He spotted the man looking down at him and the dwarf grinned before giving a rather stately bow. "May I come inside?" he asked when he straightened up. "I've got urgent news for you!"

"Are you a citizen of Carcosa?" the man yelled down. His voice was cool and somewhat emotionless but it was the tone of a man that was used to command.

"No, I'm not... My name is Ty Barron and I come from Sovereign City." His grin broadened. "Just like you."

"You know me?" the man asked.

"How could I not know the famous Lazarus Gray?" Barron pointed up at Gray and added, "But you are not the *only* Lazarus Gray - did you know that? In fact, there's another Lazarus on his way here right now."

Lazarus paused, pondering the other man's words... Lazarus Gray. He had almost forgotten his own name, though memories of his past life had often teased him, encouraging him to not give up hope, to continue to look for a way back. He thought of that woman from so long ago, the one that had told him that she feared she was just the memory of another and he felt a brief surge of fear rush through him: *Maybe that's all I am. Maybe that 'other' Lazarus is the real one...*

A strange howling sound filled the air and Lazarus saw Barron looking around with concern. "Again," the dwarf said, "I'd like to come inside. It's a bit dangerous out here..."

Lazarus studied the figure below and he came to the conclusion that this Barron, despite his ludicrous attire, was a genuine danger. He had the look about him of one skilled in the arts of deception and murder. Nevertheless, he had information that Lazarus needed.

Without another word, Lazarus spun about and moved downstairs. He yanked open the door so quickly that Barron jumped a bit in surprise. "Come in," he said to the dwarf, "and quickly tell me that you know of the other... me."

BARRON LOOKED AROUND the spartan interior, barely able to hide his disgust. It stank of sweat and piss - he couldn't imagine spending a week in a hovel like this, let alone years. It was no wonder that there was a slight look of madness in the eyes of this Lazarus Gray. "Nice place," he said, glancing in vain to see if he could find a clean place to sit. Not wanting to ruin his attire, he simply stood as Lazarus sat down on the earthen floor.

He began his tale, telling Lazarus what he had learned from the King in Yellow... of a fallen hero that had become a betrayer and killer of friends. He made no mention of The King in Yellow, however, banking on Lazarus being too engrossed in the tale to even consider how Barron had learned all of this.

"He comes to kill you," Barron said. "For you are the lost piece of him... and he fears that you may eventually return to bedevil him. Once you are gone, he will be free to embrace his new life with *your* wife and *your* son." The emphasis he placed on 'your' was not lost on Lazarus and they had their intended effect: Lazarus was filled with jealousy and rage at all that his other self had done. He didn't ask for proof because he felt the truth of it all... deep within himself, he was still somewhat tethered to his other self. Those awful things had actually been performed and they had been done by someone wearing his face and using his hands.

"How could he - how could I - have done those things?" he asked aloud, unaware that he was voicing questions already predicted by the King in Yellow.

Parroting the answers he'd been given, Murderboy lowered his voice and said, "You are the truest part of Lazarus Gray... you are the conscience that would have stopped him from putting those awful plans into place. Without you, he's just the brilliant side of you given free reign without any moral compunction. You have to destroy him and return to Earth so that you can begin to undo all the damage he's done."

Lazarus suddenly stared hard at his uninvited guest. "Kill him... that's absurd. To destroy an *aspect* of myself would be to destroy *all* of me. No. We must return to being one entity."

"No!" Barron shouted. He quickly regained control over himself and added, "I mean, it's too late for that. It's been years, Lazarus. He's been without you for so long that he's a singular being now. You are separate men now!"

Lazarus looked away, uncertainty gripping him. He knew that Barron was a liar and, further, he had seen the sudden panic that had gripped the dwarf when Lazarus had implied merging with his other self. On the other hand, such a long separation might have actually made a reunion very difficult, if not impossible.

"How long?" Lazarus asked aloud. "How long before the other me arrives?"

The dwarf barely restrained a giggle. "He should be here... any second."

———— ❈ ————

LAZARUS GRAY'S RETURN to Carcosa was anything but dignified. The portal that Catalyst and Abby had opened had seemed simple enough on Earth - a circular hole ringed by magical fire, Lazarus had merely stepped through the center. In Carcosa, however, the portal was some twelve feet in the air, located right above a muddy pit filled with three-foot long, shrimp-like creatures. Lazarus immediately dropped into this messy hole, sending the quasi-shrimp scrambling.

Lazarus emerged shaking his arms to free them of the gunk. He wondered if the unseemly arrival was the result of Nathaniel's relative inexperience or if Abby's lingering anger had caused her to drop him in the mud. Either way, he knew it was nothing less than he deserved.

He looked around, taking in the surroundings. He'd hoped to never see this place again... when last he'd come here, he had been afraid that he'd never make it back. Apparently, that fear had been a valid one since a part of him hadn't come home with him.

It was dark now, with the oversized moon hanging limp in the sky. The scent immediately came back to him, an acrid odor of decay. A lesser man would have shivered at that smell, which spoke of nothing less than the victory of age over all... the breakdown of human flesh and crumbling of stone walls. In the end, everything in Carcosa was reduced to dirt and rubble.

What would happen when he found this other 'him?' Would he readily agree to the reunion? Or would he have evolved to some state where the thought of uniting would bring about only stress and violence?

And even if Lazarus got his soul restored, would it really make any difference? Would he return to Earth only to find that his friends and family couldn't stop looking at him as a liar and murderer? Maybe it would be best to just stay here... let the ticking clock wind down and the portal close. It might be nicer for all involved. Kelly would find someone new, someone worthy of her... and Morgan would take over as leader of Assistance Unlimited, restoring the group to its status as a loving family.

Just as despair threatened to overwhelm him, the steely core of resolve that had driven him to so many victories throughout the years hardened once more. Even if he were half the man he used to be, he was still incapable of surrender... he would fight for his friends, for his life, and for his dream until there was nothing left to do. He had survived betrayal by the Illuminati, he had clawed his way out of Hell, and he had faced down the likes of Doctor Satan and the King in Yellow... he would not fall to his knees in defeat just because the path would not be easy.

Lazarus saw the tower up ahead and was grateful that he didn't have to find a way to cross the monster-infested lake. He began moving towards it, trying to ignore the squelching of mud in his shoes.

As he neared the tower, the front door opened and two men emerged - Lazarus paused, momentarily taken aback by the sight of each of them. One looked a lot like himself, though far more haggard and sporting a ratty-looking beard and long hair that trailed past his shoulders.

Both incarnations - Lazarus and Carcosa Lazarus - locked eyes for a moment. It was almost like some unseen energy was transferred from on to the other and then back again. Each felt a sudden surge of strength from the mere sight of the other... but each was also reminded just how weak they were when apart. How, they wondered, had they managed to survive for so long with only half a soul?

The outlandish figure alongside Carcosa Lazarus was quite recognizable but Lazarus couldn't fathom why he was here. It was Ty Barron, the so-called Little Lord Murderboy. The dwarf was a few feet behind Carcosa Lazarus and it seemed that he somehow sensed the energy going back and forth between the two versions of Lazarus -- and the criminal didn't approve. He looked from one to the other and his expression became one of pure disgust. As Lazarus watched, the man reached a small hand into the folds of his ludicrous clothing and pulled out a small snub-nosed pistol.

A cold burst of fear suddenly bloomed inside the heart of Lazarus Gray. He had come here to find the missing piece of himself and bond with it -- and the search had been a remarkably short one. Whatever Little Lord Murderboy had in mind for that gun, however, it couldn't bode well for either version of Lazarus.

Lazarus drew his .357 Smith & Wesson Magnum, hoping that the mud hasn't managed to gum up its works. He stopped in place, seeing the other version of himself tense up at the sight of the Magnum. Lazarus wasn't sure at first if the Carcosa Lazarus was aware that Murderboy was armed -- and what happened next convinced him that he wasn't: the dwarf raised his gun, pointing the barrel at the Carcosa Lazarus.

"There's one way to make sure that you two won't merge!" Murderboy shouted.

"No!" Lazarus shouted, quickly taking aim at the dwarf. His reflexes were far quicker than that of his enemy but the distance between them was too great. Even as Lazarus pulled the trigger, he knew that he would never be able to save the other version of himself...

Carcosa Lazarus started to whirl about, his eyes widening, but there was too little time for him to attempt to bat the gun away. Murderboy's fingers closed on the trigger at the same time as Lazarus fired his Magnum. Both shots were perfectly on target: Carcosa Lazarus's brains exploded outward in an explosion of brain matter and bone while Murderboy's diminutive form flew backwards as a bullet lodged in his heart.

Lazarus broke into a run, reaching the two fallen men with just a few hurried steps. He dropped to his knees beside the other version of himself but even before inspecting the body that was so much like his own, he knew it was pointless. Muderboy's bullet had passed right through the Carcosa Lazarus's skull... and with his doppleganger's death, so too had gone any chance of restoring himself to normality.

The hot sting of tears began to fill the hero's eyes as he realized that he had failed. He could never go home now, not like this.. the bizarre notion of simply lying to them all came unbidden to his mind but he pushed it away. That kind of thinking was too much like the sort that had led to all of this trouble in the first place.

No, it was better to simply surrender to the inevitable. He had lost his only chance at possible redemption. It was over.

⸻

"**N**OT QUITE, MON ami."

Lazarus sprang to his feet and spun about, bringing his gun to bear. Standing there was the purple-garbed figure named L'Homme Fantastique. Lazarus lowered his pistol and asked, "How did you get here?"

"I am a mysterious fellow, no?" He stepped around the two corpses, careful not to let his expensive shoes come too close to the spreading pools of red. "I have a patron that was able to dispatch me here without your friends being the wiser... A pity about your other self. It's a good thing that I managed to capture that last remnant of soul before it vanished entirely."

"You did what?"

L'Homme Fantastique held up a small bottle containing an emerald mist. As Lazarus stared at it, he was startled to see a face take shape within the cloudy mixture - and he recognized the screaming features of himself. "This is the other part of your soul - all it would take is for you to dump the contents of this down your throat and you would be restored."

Lazarus shifted his weight from one foot to the other. "I notice that you aren't handing it over... is this when you reveal that you've been Doctor Satan all along? Or are you really who you appear to be... but now you want to bargain with me?"

L'Homme Fantastique removed his hat, revealing his smudged features. "It would be quite the twist for me to be Satan, non? Unfortunately, I truly am the being that I've always claimed to be -- and you and I have incomplete business."

Lazarus nodded, reading between the lines. "We have to play the game... so you can judge whether or not I live or die." He looked down at his Magnum. "I assume this gun wouldn't have any effect on you otherwise you wouldn't have approached me so closely."

"You are a smart one, mon ami. You are right on both counts - I am immune to your bullets and oui, we shall play a game. If you win, then this vial will be given to you. You'll be restored to your true spiritual state. If you lose, then I smash the vial and you shall never be free of this realm. You will live here until your form slowly dissipates into madness and unbeing."

"And if I *am* restored... there's no guarantee that my friends will forgive me, is there?"

L'Homme Fantastique chuckled. "You are a worry-wart in this form! They will forgive you - they are desperate to do it! All they need is to see the real you again and they will know - they will *know* - that you're back." Growing more serious, L'Homme Fantastique placed a gloved hand on Gray's shoulder. "You are a lucky man. They love you so very much."

A pair of mismatched eyes stared into the Frenchman's smudged features - brown and green, they seemed like the eyes of two men forced into one head. L'Homme Fantastique thought that those eyes symbolized so very much... how Richard Winthrop had become Lazarus Gray; how Lazarus himself had been split into two; and how Sovereign City itself could simultaneously be a town filled with the seediest of people... and the most stalwart of warriors.

When Lazarus spoke, L'Homme Fantastique was freed from the

spell of those eyes. He had never experienced anything quite like it and he was a bit shaken as Lazarus asked, "What are we waiting for?"

"All I need is for you to say oui -- yes," L'Homme Fantastique stammered.

With a definitive nod, Lazarus said, "Let's play."

"HE'S GONE!" KELLY was pacing around the room, her eyes wide. She brushed off Samantha's grip when the other woman tried to touch her arm. The assembled heroes of Assistance Unlimited were gathered around a floating rift of energy in the center of the room - the passage to Carcosa. "Didn't you hear me? He's pulling some trick!"

"Maybe he is and maybe he's not," Samantha said, glancing over at Abby. "There's nothing we can do about it, is there?"

Abby paused before answering. "Well, I can try to see if I can find him anywhere in the city... looking throughout the world might be pretty time-consuming, though. To be honest, I wouldn't expect to find him at all. If I had to guess, I'd think he managed to get into Carcosa on his own. He certainly didn't go through the portal."

"I'm so dumb," Kelly muttered. "He's going to interfere somehow. I knew he was out to get Lazarus and I let him stay around here anyway!" She froze in place and put a hand over her mouth.

"Stop beating yourself up," The Black Terror said. "Without him, we wouldn't have gotten Catalyst here and we wouldn't have been able to open the portal. We needed him. If he's betraying us now, all we can do is hope that Lazarus can best him. Personally, I'm not betting against Laz."

"We need to decide how we're going to handle things if Lazarus does come back," Morgan said with a grim tone. "Is it forgive and forget after all the things he did?"

THE LIFE AND DEATH AND LIFE OF LAZARUS GRAY

Kelly stared at Morgan with ice in her expression. "There's no 'if he comes back,' Morgan. He *is* coming back. And when he does, he's going to be the way he used to be. This... person... that hurt you and everyone else wasn't the real him."

"She's right," Samantha said. "I know this isn't necessarily true for all the people in The Heroes but the core Assistance Unlimited folks... Lazarus saved us all. He picked us up from the gutter -- literally and figuratively. He never gave up on us and we shouldn't do that to him. So, yes, Morgan... I'm going to forgive, even if I can't forget." She turned towards her friend and put her hands on her hips, as if daring him to tell that she was wrong.

"So am I," Eun said, taking off his cap and running his hand through his hair. "I'm just gonna think of it like he was possessed or something. It happens." He looked over at Blue Fire, who was watching him with amazement. "If you're in the hero biz for a few more years, pal, you'll know exactly what I mean."

Morgan paused, smoothing down the edges of his moustache. When he spoke, he nodded and replied, "You're right... no matter what he did, he's Lazarus Gray. He's our friend." Glancing over at Samantha, who was still glaring at him in a challenging fashion, he added, "You can relax, Sam. I'm on your side."

While the various heroes were coming to the same conclusion, one figure slowly slipped out of the room, letting the door latch close so quietly that no one realized what he had done. El Demonio had been freed by The Heroes in case he would be needed to battle Assistance Unlimited and in the end, it had turned out to be an unnecessary maneuver. Yes, they had gone so far as to give him his own chair in their headquarters but he had no doubt that they would soon seek to throw him back into Tartarus.

For the masked villain, this whole affair was proof that he was not meant to waste away in a prison cell... instead, he would return home and reclaim his criminal empire. He was willing to toss aside thoughts of revenge against Eun and his companions, at least for now. Becoming lord and master of the Mexican underworld was his overriding goal. It would not be easy and would require many battles and much bloodshed...

El Demonio's heart pounded in excitement. He couldn't wait to begin.

———∞∞∞———

THE FRENCHMAN SAT down on a rock that had been weathered by the environment into a dome-like shape. He pulled off his gloves and set them down beside his feet and then he held out one of his hands to Lazarus. Where it had been empty seconds before, there were now two small wooden cubes in the palm of his hand, roughly hewn to resemble dice. Each of them was marked on six sides and Lazarus studied the designs as his opponent shifted his hand, allowing the dice to roll across his palm: the symbols were I, II, III, X, +, and #.

L'Homme Fantastique gestured for Lazarus to take a seat and Assistance Unlimited's leader did so, sitting on his knees across from the Frenchman. There was a flat, bare piece of earth between them.

"This dice game is played by the Negritos of the Zambales region of the Philippines," L'Homme Fantastique explained. "It is typically played with wagers attached - often for small items such as camotes, tobacco leaves or rough-made cigars."

Lazarus spoke up and his words caused L'Homme Fantastique to sit back in surprise. "I'm familiar with the game, actually. I read *Negritos of Zambales, Volume 2, Parts 1-3* during my time with The Illuminati. If I recall correctly, it's described in detail on page 49[10]."

"Impressive memory."

Lazarus leaned forward and replied, "My recollection isn't always perfect but I've trained my mind to retain most bits of information. The basic rules are that we each have five chances to throw the two dice. If one of us pairs the dice, we 'win' and gain a point. After we've taken five throws, the one with the most points is declared the winner. If we end up with equal points, it's a draw and neither of us lose anything."

The Frenchman nodded eagerly. "Oui! But I think that since our time is running late, we will limit ourselves to three throws each, instead

10 Not surprisingly, Lazarus is correct! The book was published in 1904.

of the usual five. If you win, I give you this missing piece of your soul and we return to Earth. If I win, I smash the vial, preventing you from ever being restored to the man you were… and for the safety of all involved, I shall leave you here in Carcosa."

"And if it's a draw…?" Lazarus asked.

"Then we keep playing until we have a winner, mon ami." L'Homme Fantastique offered the dice to Lazarus and said, "We shall parler while we play."

Lazarus took the dice and began to shake them in his closed hand. He waited until he felt the time was right and let the dice play. They bounced across the smooth ground, finally landing with a II and a + facing upward. "Your turn, Fantastique."

The Frenchman plucked up the dice with a swipe of a hand and he sounded genuinely curious when he asked, "Were you not tempted to stay with The Illuminati after you found out the truth? You had fought alongside them for years… your mentor, Walther Lunt, was almost a second father to you… and your lover, Miya Shimada, was a devout member that no doubt begged you to stay.."

Lazarus paused as L'Homme Fantastique threw the dice: a I and III. "Of course I was tempted. I knew that they were a dangerous organization and that turning against them would be a foolhardy choice. And, as you pointed out, I would be losing my closest friends. I tried to convince both of them to rebel alongside me but I quickly realized that Walther had always planned to subvert me to the Illuminati cause and that Miya was running a badger game. Her feelings for me were never real."

Fantastique sat back as Lazarus prepared for his second roll. "I'm curious - after being betrayed by so many… why would you immediately begin surrounding yourself with others? Most men would have been unlikely to trust anyone so soon."

Lazarus tossed the game pieces and resisted the urge to frown as he once again missed matching a pair. This time he got an X and a #. "It wasn't a deliberate decision," Lazarus answered. "After I founded Assistance Unlimited as a one-man operation, I adopted the name

Lazarus Gray in hopes of drawing out someone that might be able to answer the questions I had about my past--"

"You had amnesia after The Illuminati tried to kill you?"

"That's right. Anyway, one of the first people that I helped was Morgan Watts. I recognized that circumstances had led him to become a criminal but that his heart wasn't it. The seed of goodness was inside him, just waiting to be nurtured. So I asked him to join me and he became my first agent."

"It didn't bother you that he had killed people in service to crimelords? That he had been to jail multiple times?" L'Homme Fantastique's second toss of the dice resulted in a II but the second dice looked like it might fall in a match but flipped one last time to land on a I.

"A man's past actions don't define his existence. If I didn't believe in the possibility of redemption, I wouldn't have built Tartarus... I would simply gun down my enemies. Morgan is a good man -- he's proven that over and over again. All he needed was someone to believe in him."

Fantastique nodded thoughtfully. "Yet the one you called Eidolon... you eventually asked him to leave the group, did you not?"

Lazarus held the dice in his hand, shaking them before answering. "Yes. The first time he left it was of his own accord... then he returned and we welcomed him back with open arms. He and Bob decided to operate outside of our missions and outside of our rules. They were excessively violent. When I confronted them, I gave both the opportunity to stay or go, the choice was theirs. If they remained, they had to swear off the violence. Bob agreed to do so but Josef refused... so we let him walk."

"Would you give him another chance if he asked for it?" Fantastique asked, lowering his voice.

After a pause, Lazarus nodded. "I would. He was part of our family. I'd never turn my back on him completely."

"Everyone makes mistakes, oui? Some are just bigger than others."

"That's right," Lazarus agreed. "Sovereign City has been ruled by corruption for so long... Assistance Unlimited is there to show everyone that no matter what you've done, no matter what you've put up with for far too long, you can do better. You have to be given the chance and you have to take that chance. It goes both ways."

"I think I see."

Lazarus let the dice go. They bounced high, clacking as they smacked into one another. One landed smoothly, an X facing upward. The second spun about on one of its points... before finally coming down with a matching X on its surface.

L'Homme Fantastique was already in the midst of handing Lazarus the vial containing the other half of his soul. "Congratulations, Monsieur Gray."

"You haven't taken your third and final throw," Lazarus pointed out.

"That is true," L'Homme Fantastique confirmed. "But I concede the defeat - today the dice are not my friends."

"This... game... of yours," Lazarus asked, looking down at the vial that he now held gingerly in his grip. "It's not really chance at all, is it? You determine the winner based upon the answers a player gives."

L'Homme Fantastique stood up and shrugged. "I believe that good things happen to good people. You were honest and good-hearted in your words and deeds so the dice went your way. Congratulations." He turned to leave and said over his shoulder, "Perhaps we will meet again, Monsieur Gray... though I doubt it. Once a man has won a game from me, I rarely seek them out again. Give your lovely wife my regards."

Watching Fantastique walk away into the mist, Lazarus felt a rush of excitement. There was so much to be ashamed of but the first step to atonement literally lay in his grasp. He uncorked the vial and poured its contents down his throat. It felt like inhaling candle smoke and he coughed once as the gaseous form rushed down into his core.

For a moment, his vision swam and he felt weak in the knees... then a rush of strength washed over him and he stood tall, feeling a sense of confidence that he hadn't felt in years. Gone was the sense of doubt that had become so familiar to him that he'd stopped noticing it... he knew what he had to do and he was fully aware that it would be a difficult path to walk… but he was firmly convinced that he could accomplish his goal.

Once again, like his namesake, Lazarus had risen anew.

CHAPTER XIV
EVERYTHING IN ITS PLACE

MAJOR JOSHUA CARUSO was tall, with the sort of rangy build commonly found among polo players or swimmers. His hair was a reddish-blond and cut short, though a few strands of it fell over his forehead in a calculatingly haphazard fashion. He wore a blue suit, white shirt and striped tie, all of which looked like they'd been custom-tailored to his specifications. There was an air of regal breeding about him but he was no soft scion of nobility - there was a hint of danger in his eyes and an obvious love of adventure.

As head of the United States' answer to Germany's Occult Forces Project, Caruso was frequently exposed to the bizarre: he had a team of psychics that worked for his agency; he had recently sat in on a seance to try and get military tactical support from no less than George Washington himself; and he had spent altogether too much time for his liking in the presence of Lazarus Gray and Assistance Unlimited. His was a peculiar career and one that had resulted in his own sister being terrorized by a killer known as Billhook... but despite all of this, he relished his work as the head of Project: Cicada.

Project: Cicada had reluctantly been signed into operation by no less than the President himself - FDR had been hesitant because his Christian beliefs condemned much of the supernatural as being demonic in origin and he had no desire for the United States to go down that path. Caruso and others had pointed out the success that the Germans had found with the OFP, including the creation of multiple superhuman agents. The United States had plenty of superhumans - more than any other nation on Earth - but the vast majority of them operated without government oversight. Even the likes of The Fighting Yank occasionally made moves that rankled those in Washington… and attempts to create heroes that would 'belong' to the U.S. government had mostly proven failures: either the experiments didn't succeed or those that were produced bolted from their controllers at some point, as The Black Terror had done. The Brits had managed to achieve a modicum of success with their own endeavours, having created the man known as Intrepid… but he was a lone agent and it wasn't likely that the Brits would loan him out to the U.S. of A for any length of time[11].

Caruso exited his vehicle, briefcase in hand, and approached 6196 Robeson Avenue with caution. He knew that the entire city block was owned by Lazarus Gray but one wouldn't know it from the unassuming appearance of the surroundings. . What had once been a quiet neighborhood had been transformed into the beating heart of Gray's law-abiding enterprise.

The centerpiece of his holdings was a three-story structure that had once been a hotel. Gray's associates used the first floor, while the second had been gutted and converted into one large room that was used for meetings, briefings, and research. The third floor was off-limits to everyone but Lazarus and his family, serving as their private residence. He lived there with his wife Kelly and their three-year-old son Ezekiel.

Facing the former hotel were several storefronts, all of which had closed down at the dawn of the Great Depression. They were now quite empty, though each was equipped with sensitive monitoring equipment that allowed Lazarus and his companions to keep track of every car or pedestrian that stepped foot onto Robeson Avenue.

Right on cue, one of the doors along the front entrance to the building swung open, revealing the smiling face of Abigail Cross. The pretty brunette wore a figure-hugging green dress that was cinched at the waist and which featured a plunging neckline, revealing enough décolletage to momentarily distract the military officer.

"Major Caruso - it's good to see you again." Abby positioned her back against the door so she could offer a hand to Caruso. To her surprise and amusement, the Major didn't give it a polite squeeze but rather lifted it so that his lips brushed against her knuckles.

11 Don't worry if you haven't heard of Intrepid before - just stay tuned and you'll learn plenty about him in the future.

"The pleasure, as always, is mine, Miss Cross."

"I've never noticed that you were so gallant," Abby said, her eyes shining.

Caruso stepped into the building and waited for her as the door fell shut. "To be honest, I was in a relationship before. Not a very steady one but an occasional thing… anyway, until I was completely free of it, I didn't feel it was proper to let you know of my interest."

"And that's what you're doing now? Showing me your interest?"

"I'm trying to," Caruso admitted. They walked down the hall, towards the meeting room where the Major had been on several occasions. "Would you like to have dinner with me tonight?"

Abby pursed her full lips in a thoughtful manner. "I think I'm free. What time did you want to pick me up?"

"How about seven?"

"I'll be waiting," Abby replied. "Formal?"

"I wouldn't be much of a gentleman if I didn't try to impress a lady on the first date."

"I'll dress appropriately, then," she said with a twinkle in her eye.

Caruso was smiling like he'd just won the lottery when they stepped into the meeting room. He recognized the faces staring back at him but he thought he detected a tension there that usually wasn't present.

Seated around the table were Lazarus Gray, his wife Kelly, Morgan Watts, Eun Jiwon, The Black Terror, and Samantha Grace. Resting on the table in front of Lazarus was a medium-sized wooden crate. It was unmarked but something about the box kept drawing Caruso's eyes back towards it.

"Having a good day, Major?" Lazarus asked.

Caruso waited until Abby had gone around the table and taken her seat before he accepted the remaining chair. "It didn't start out particularly well but I just received some good news." Before anyone could inquire further, the military man asked, "So why did you call me here? Does it have something to do with the box on the table?"

"It does, actually," Lazarus confirmed. He stood up, looking dapper in his suit and tie. Caruso detected the tell-tale bulge of a gun holstered beneath the man's jacket but he wasn't surprised - as far as he knew, Assistance Unlimited's leader slept with the damned thing under his pillow at night. Removing the lid of the box, Lazarus reached in and pushed aside some straw. He held up something that had been protectively packed inside - a human bone, one that Caruso recognized as being a femur. "These, Lazarus continued, "are the last remains of Doctor Satan."

That caught Caruso's full attention. "He's dead? You're sure it's him…? I've heard so many false reports of his death…"

"These are his bones," Lazarus confirmed. "I was there when he died and I was the one that threw his body into a vat of acid." When Caruso started to speak, Lazarus said, "It's a long story. Suffice to say, he died… but that doesn't mean he can't return. He's not a normal man."

"So I've heard. Originally we thought he might be a spoiled rich boy out for some sadistic kicks but time has proven otherwise." Caruso watched as Lazarus dropped the femur back among the straw. Caruso noticed as Lazarus re-packed the contents that he saw Satan's skull in the box, complete with tiny horns growing from the bone. After clearing his throat, he asked, "How do we stop him from… resurrecting?"

Lazarus glanced at Abby and nodded. She said, "I've confirmed that his essence is still tied to the bones. There are a number of spells that could be used to bring him back to life. To try and reduce the chance of that succeeding, I've put some magical wards on the box."

"I don't see anything," Caruso confessed.

"That's because you're not a warlock," Morgan muttered. "For what it's worth, I don't see anything either."

"We want you to take the box," Lazarus said and Caruso blinked in surprise.

"I thought that's why you guys had Tartarus…"

"Tartarus is designed to hold living prisoners. It's not a storehouse for the obscene or dangerous items that we collect. Some of those we've kept around this building but since you have a larger operation than we do, I think it's time we turned some of them over to you... not all of them, of course." Lazarus locked those mismatched eyes of his onto Caruso and said in a steady voice, "We've come to trust you, Major, but you could be removed from your position at any time and there are some things in our possession that we wouldn't want being turned into weapons."

"Understood," Caruso replied. "I'll put this someplace safe... and I'll leave its existence off the official books so nobody in Washington will find out about it and come sniffing around." After Lazarus had put the lid back in place, Caruso slid the box closer to himself and added, "Any other business?"

"Actually, yes." Lazarus took his seat once more and said, "I know that Project: Cicada ran background checks on all of us before you asked us to form a working relationship with you."

Caruso shifted uneasily, casting a quick glance at a frowning Eun. Those files had been used against Assistance Unlimited at one point, with all of their darkest secrets being released to the press. Eun in particular had been furious to have his homosexuality exposed. "I can assure you that we're not monitoring your group any more, Lazarus."

"We're adding a new member and I thought you might want to," Lazarus replied. "I know how the government works and having Cicada's backing has greased the wheels of bureaucracy a few times for us so I don't want to have anything cause a problem there."

"That's a good idea," Caruso admitted. "Who's the new member?"

Samantha sprang up and hurried over to open the door. Caruso watched as a handsome man entered - he looked vaguely familiar to the Major and he suddenly realized why: he had recently read a newspaper clipping concerning the man's vigilante activities.

"Blue Fire?" Caruso asked, leaning over the table to offer a hand.

Jack Richard Knapp returned a firm handshake. "Nice to meet you, sir. Mr. Gray says that you're part of a Top Secret operation?" There was a noticeable glimmer of excitement in Knapp's voice when he asked the question, which brought a smile to Caruso's face.

"That's true." Caruso looked at the enthusiastic young man and asked, "I thought you were a West Coast guy -- how did you end up here in Sovereign?"

"It's kind of a long story, sir," Jack replied, looking somewhat sheepish. It was clear to Caruso that whatever the tale was, Jack wasn't anxious to share it at the moment.

Lazarus spoke up, saying, "We have a spinoff group known as The Heroes, mostly based in New York. Jack here is going to be staying with us as part of a... peer review process."

Eun let out a grunt of amusement but he kept a straight face when Caruso glanced his way. "Well, we'll make sure that Mr. Knapp is cleared for duty - Did I get your hero name right? Is it Blue Fire or Blue Flame?"

"You got it right the first time - Blue Fire," Jack answered.

"Got it." Caruso turned back to Lazarus. "What else?"

Lazarus shifted a bit in his chair, as if hesitant to speak. With a bit of surprise, Caruso realized that the man was actually embarrassed - a trait that he'd never seen in Lazarus before. "I'm stepping down as leader of Assistance Unlimited, at least for a brief time."

"You're leaving the group?" Caruso asked in shock.

"Not at all - we've agreed, however, that it's time for Morgan to handle the administrative side of things. He'll be leaving fieldwork and staying here, coordinating our efforts and making sure that things run smoothly."

"That's another reason for Jack here to join the team," Morgan said. "He'll ensure that we aren't short-handed."

Caruso grunted and said, "Actually... I was kind of glad to get an invitation to come here because I was hoping to get one of you guys to join a mission of ours that will go behind enemy lines. It might last a couple of months and I think it will definitely require someone with... unusual... abilities."

"That rules out most of us," Samantha answered.

Morgan leaned forward thoughtfully and Caruso was again struck by how incongruous this scene seemed to be - he wasn't used to seeing anyone other than Lazarus calling the shots. "I don't think it would be wise to send off Jack when he's so new to us," Morgan said, "and Abby's needed here for her magical expertise and to oversee Tartarus. That leaves Bob... not that we wouldn't miss you, of course."

The Black Terror shrugged his shoulders, showing he took no offense. "I wouldn't mind getting a chance to cut loose. I don't like to unleash my full strength on gangsters if I can help it - but some Nazis? Them I can beat up on without any guilt. I'll need a little bit of time to make sure that Tim can stay with Jean but once that's taken care of, I'll be free to go."

"Great." Caruso looked once more at the box containing the remains of Doctor Satan. "So is that it? Satan's dead, Morgan's in charge, Bob's headed to Europe, and Blue Fire is going to be hanging around Sovereign?"

"I believe that covers it all," Lazarus agreed.

Morgan stood up and offered a hand. "Thanks for coming, Major. We'll be in touch - and if you need us, don't hesitate to call."

"Don't let the stress of being chief get you down, Morgan." Caruso winked as he offered the advice and Morgan grinned in response. The major locked eyes with Abby for a brief moment before hefting the box of bones in his arms and carrying it from the room.

As soon as their visitor was gone, the various members of Assistance Unlimited began to rise and engage in conversations: Eun and Bob were talking about the renovation project that would soon be commencing, as the 'cloning chamber' was going to be converted into a small gymnasium; Samantha was quizzing Abigail about the looks she'd spotted flowing between Abby and Caruso; Kelly invited Jack to join her in a tour of the facility; and Lazarus looked at Morgan and whispered, "You're going to do fine."

"If you say so," Morgan answered with a sigh. "I get why you're doing this and I'd be a liar if I didn't say it went a long way in making us all trust you again… but I think you'd have been a smarter guy to have put somebody else in charge. Unless it's really just a way to get the old man out of the field…"

"You're the best man for the job," Lazarus retorted.

"No, I'm not," Morgan said firmly. He turned to face his friend and added, "You're the best person for this - you always have been and you always will be. And someday the job's going to be yours again." Before Lazarus could respond, Morgan had wrapped him into an embrace.

The conversations around them fell silent and, without anyone saying anything, the entire room converged upon the two men at its center. The group engaged in a large hug and for a moment the members of Assistance Unlimited seemed to exist as one organism, living and breathing in unison.

And at the core of this ever-shifting group was Lazarus Gray, a man forever dying and being reborn, both literally and figuratively.

EPILOGUE

October 1943

TIM ROLAND COULDN'T sleep. He knew that he should be resting up but the idea that his mentor and surrogate father was off in Germany without him made him restless. He sat up in bed and ran a hand through his short-trimmed hair. It was almost always an unruly mess but the girls seemed to like it so Tim had never worried over it. In the few years since he'd come to live with Bob, he'd often wondered if someone would put two-and-two together and figure out his identity… but it hadn't happened so far.

To the world at large, Bob Benton was a mild-mannered… almost cowardly… pharmacist. Tim was a street urchin made good, excelling at school and apprenticing in chemistry under Bob's watchful eyes. What hardly anyone knew was that Tim frequently sported a black outfit adorned with a skull and crossbones, just like The Black Terror's. Though few people paid him enough attention to even wonder what he was called, Tim had taken to identifying himself as Black Terror, Junior… but mostly Bob just called him Tim and the press just referred to them both as the Terror Twins. Their adventures had been fictionalized into comic books and pulp novels but until recently they hadn't been very accurate - now that Assistance Unlimited was letting this Fitzgerald character handle most of the pulp stuff, the quality was a whole lot better.

Tim slid out from under the covers and crept towards the door. He listened for a moment until he was certain that Jean Starr wasn't moving about downstairs. He shared an apartment above the pharmacy with Bob

- Jean had volunteered to keep tabs on Tim while Bob was away at what she thought was a conference. She was aware of their secret identities but she still had a tendency to worry so Bob often kept her in the dark about his missions.

Hearing nothing, Tim stepped out and wandered downstairs. He was in his pajamas and he shivered slightly in the autumn chill. Jean had gone home, locking the place up and leaving out a small plate of cookies for Tim. He grinned and snatched one up, munching happily.

As he ate, he noticed that the flame in one of the many gas lanterns that Bob kept around the office was still lit. Bob liked the old-fashioned lighting methods and frequently saved on electricity by using the lanterns while working at night.

It was unlike Jean to leave one of the lanterns on and Tim blew it out, cookie still in hand. As he turned away from it, the flame reappeared, blossoming to life once more.

A chill went down Tim's spine as he stared at the flickering light. There seemed to be shapes forming within it, tiny human figures… a man and a woman. The figures suddenly jumped in size and two full-sized human beings suddenly emerged from the fire, landing on their feet just in front of Tim.

To say that they were a wondrous sight would have been an understatement. The man wore a yellow suit with scarlet gloves and boots and his face was hidden behind a crimson mask. A long red cloak hung off his shoulders. On the center of his chest was the image of a flame and in his right hand was a strange pistol of some kind.

The woman was beautiful, with long blonde hair that fell in ringlets down her shoulders. She was dressed in a red blouse and miniskirt that revealed an ample amount of leg. A domino mask and small hat completed the outfit and, like the man, she was armed. A standard handgun was clutched in her left hand.

The man studied Tim closely and quickly holstered his gun. He nodded at the woman to do the same and, with obvious reluctance, she followed suit.

"Son… are you the one called Black Terror, Junior?"

Tim couldn't help but smile… someone had been paying attention! He hesitated a moment, unsure if he should reveal his identity, but finally nodded. If these two had come this far, they probably had figured out Bob's connection to the Terror. "That's me," he said. "Who are you two?"

"I'm called The Flame… but you might as well know me by my real name: Gary Preston. This is Miss Masque."

Tim's eyes widened. He was familiar with both of them and had, in fact, entered information on them in The Black Terror's Heroic Compendium, a sort of encyclopedia that Bob was amassing on various mystery men. There were entries on all the major heroes: the Peregrine, Leonid Kaslov, the Black Bat, Intrepid and many more.

Miss Masque nudged The Flame, mischief in her voice. "I think he's heard of us."

"Of course I have!" Tim blurted out. "You're Diana Adams, a socialite who turned to fighting crime to erase the boredom she was feeling! And Gary Preston's father was a missionary in China when he died in a flood. Gary was just an infant but when he was washed into a hidden land, the Buddhists who lived there proclaimed him a High Grand Lama and taught him to control flame!"

Miss Masque crossed her arms over her chest. "How do you know all that? And why do you talk like you're reciting something you read in a book?"

"Sorry… Bob and I got most of that information from The Peregrine. He's been helping us put together a dossier on all the heroes who are active right now."

"And how the hell did he find out who I really am?" Miss Masque demanded but The Flame touched her arm.

"Diana, let it go." The Flame smiled at Tim. "Listen, son, is The Black Terror around?"

"No. He's in Germany on a secret mission for Project: Cicada."

Miss Masque turned away, looking around the pharmacy. She had never warmed up to kids... not even when she'd been one. She'd always wanted to be with the grownups, to know what their parties were like... what they were talking about and whom they were seeing. Now that she was grown herself, she knew how dark a lot of that "grown up" talk really was... but it hadn't altered her feelings for children.

"Well... you'll have to do, then." The Flame reached out and clasped the young man by the shoulder. "We need help, son. And you're going to have to help provide it. The world depends on it."

"Of course I'll help... but can't it wait until The Black Terror is back?"

"I'm afraid not. Every second we waste worsens that situation. You have time to leave your mentor a brief note, though. And... tell him that if he wants to find you later on, to look for the Claws of the Peregrine."

"The Claws of the Peregrine? What's that?"

"He'll understand... when the time is right."

Tim nodded and turned away, hurrying off to find both his costume and some paper to fashion his note. When he was out of the room, Miss Masque cast a disapproving look at The Flame. "This isn't right. He's a child."

"He's got a destiny, Diana, just like you and I do."

"You should at least tell him...."

"What? That's he's about to lose out on a few years of his childhood?" Gary Preston's voice took on an edge now and Diana knew she'd touched a nerve. Gary had been on edge ever since Flame Girl's death. "This is important. You know that. If The Black Terror were here, I'd take him instead... but he's not and we don't have time to recruit Assistance Unlimited. Most of them don't have powers anyway," he added.

Miss Masque said nothing but she couldn't help but feel annoyed at Gary's callous words - she didn't have any powers and she liked to think that she'd been pretty damned useful so far. Wanting to think about something else, she wondered what The Black Terror would think when he returned and heard the words "Claws of the Peregrine."

They wouldn't make any sense to him, of course, since The Claws of the Peregrine were still nearly a year away from being formed.

"Time travel gives me such a headache," she whispered.

THE END

NEVER THE END
FROM THE AUTHOR'S FEVERED BRAIN

WOW.

This book was the hardest of the entire series for me to write, for many different reasons. I had to juggle an enormous number of characters, reference events that took place over the course of many books, and somehow bring our hero back from his very lowest point. You'll have to let me know how successful I was in pulling it off.

My shared universe is sometimes a source of strength... but it also means jumping through some continuity hoops to make sure it all lines up. Case in point: I've known for quite some time that Tim would vanish and Bob would have to leave Assistance Unlimited in an attempt to find him - these events had happened in a Peregrine story I wrote years ago but set in both 1943 & 1946 - so when this series reached late '43, I needed to make sure all those things came to pass. For a few moments during the writing of this novel I felt like one of those comic book authors whose plot is hijacked as part of a company-wide crossover... only I was the one responsible for all the continuity issues!

When I finished volume eleven and sent it to Tommy Hancock at Pro Se, I told him he might want to read the last scene right away. He did so and I still chuckle over his rather amazed reaction. He immediately - and rightly - wanted to know if I had a plan to resolve all this in a way that wouldn't ruin the property's future. I assured him that I did have a plan in mind and that by the end of volume twelve, Lazarus would have been restored in some fashion. I always knew that it would tie back in to Carcosa but I wasn't sure that I could accurately transform my thoughts into prose -- while looking over volume seven, I actually stumbled across the conversation with the woman who said that she wasn't sure if she was even a real person or just a memory of one. That caused the remaining pieces to fall into place and I knew what I wanted to do.

By the way, the scene where Lazarus almost single-handedly bests The Heroes was inspired by the moment in Marvel's original Secret

Wars series where Spider-Man does the same thing to the X-Men. I always thought it showed how much of a badass Spidey could really be and hopefully I was able to paint Lazarus in a similar light.

So where does the series go from here? I have plans for the future - by now you've seen Assistance Unlimited: The Silver Age so you know a little bit about how the AU team looks in the Sixties... but how do we get from here to there? It won't be a smooth ride, of course - if it was, it wouldn't make for very entertaining reading, now would it?

As Black Terror exits our series (bye, Bob!), you'll see Blue Fire stick around. Jack is a very obscure character but I like him - and he's got a scientific background so he'll kind of replace Bob in that regard. The transition from a superstrong bruiser to a guy that can become intangible will alter the way the team operates, too. In case you're wondering how and why I came to use Jack at all -- prepare yourself for another peek behind the curtain. R.A. Jones writes a wonderful series of books based around the Steel Ring group of heroes. At one point, I was contacted by the editor of that series and was asked if I would be interested in writing a spinoff novel. I jumped at the chance, being a fan of those books... and I was then given a list of characters and a barebones plot to work from. One of those characters was (you guessed it) Blue Fire. Unfortunately, the novel never came to true fruition and so it lies completed in the dusty catacombs of my Google Drive.

But I liked Jack... and so he made the leap from *that* series to *this* series.

Of course, there was another major addition to the series with this book, wasn't there?

What will become of L'Homme Fantastique? He has operated in Sovereign for quite some time without being noticed... so he may return to the shadows, where he'll continue to do his gimmick without being seen by most. Then again, if you guys clamor for more, I'm sure he'll pop up either here or elsewhere in the Reese Unlimited universe. Only time will tell!

Take Care,
Barry Reese
01/30/2020

THE REESE UNLIMITED TIMELINE

THE REESE UNLIMITED TIMELINE

Major Events specific to certain stories and novels are included in brackets. Some of this information contains SPOILERS for The Peregrine, Lazarus Gray, Gravedigger and other stories.

~ 800 – Viking warrior Grimarr dies of disease but is resurrected as the Sword of Hel. He adventures for some time as Hel's agent on Earth. **[The Sword of Hel]**.

~ 1620 – Gwydion fab Dôn is captured by the witch Rhianna in France. She punishes him by binding his spirit to a bundle of rags. **["Gwydion," The Adventures of the Straw-Man Volume One]**

1748 – Johann Adam Weishaupt is born.

1750 – Guan-Yin embarks on a quest to find her lost father, which takes her to Skull Island **[Guan-Yin and the Horrors of Skull Island]**.

1774 – On June 23, 1774, General Benjamin Grove led the British forces through the air en route to Sovereign. What he did not know was that several local militia groups lay in wait for him. The resulting battle had been ferocious and deadly for both sides — in the end, only two men were left, one representing each side of the conflict: General Grove himself and a local youth by the name of Emmett Hain. **["The Choice," The Adventures of the Straw-Man Volume One]**

1776 – Johann Adam Weishaupt forms The Illuminati. He adopts the guise of the original Lazarus Gray in group meetings, reflecting his "rebirth" and the "moral ambiguity" of the group. In Sovereign City, a Hessian soldier dies in battle, his spirit resurrected as a headless warrior.

1782 – The man that would eventually be known as Gideon Black is born. **[The Second Book of Babylon]**

1793 – Mortimer Quinn comes to Sovereign City, investigating the tales of a Headless Horseman **[Gravedigger Volume One]**

1802 – Gideon Black's son is born and the chain of events that leads to Gideon being bonded with a suit of armor forged in Hell begins. Gideon is transformed into Babylon, a force for cosmic retribution. **[The Second Book of Babylon]**

1835 – Lucy Hale goes to work at Mendicott Hall. She meets Byron Mendicott and Lilith. **[The Chronicles of Lilith]**

1865 – Eobard Grace returns home from his actions in the American Civil War. Takes possession of the Book of Shadows from his uncle Frederick. **["The World of Shadow," The Family Grace: An Extraordinary History]**

1877 – Eobard Grace is summoned to the World of Shadows, where he battles Uris-Kor and fathers a son, Korben. **["The World of Shadow," The Family Grace: An Extraordinary History]**

1885 – Along with his niece Miriam and her paramour Ian Sinclair, Eobard returns to the World of Shadows to halt the merging of that world with Earth. **["The Flesh Wheel," The Family Grace: An Extraordinary History]**

1890 – Eobard fathers a second son, Leopold.

1893 – Eobard Grace successfully steals the Thirty Pieces of Silver that was paid to Judas for his betrayal of Jesus from The Illuminati. He melts the coins down into mystically-empowered silver and helps a friend forge these into bullets. They remain hidden in Atlanta, Georgia until the Forties. **[The Adventures of Lazarus Gray Volume 11]**

1895 – Felix Cole (The Bookbinder) is born.

1900 – Max Davies is born to publisher Warren Davies and his wife, heiress Margaret Davies.

1901 – Leonid Kaslov is born.

1905 – Richard Winthrop is born in San Francisco.

1908 – Warren Davies is murdered by Ted Grossett, a killer nicknamed

"Death's Head". ["**Lucifer's Cage**", **the Peregrine Volume One**, more details shown in **"Origins," the Peregrine Volume One**] Hans Merkel kills his own father. ["**Blitzkrieg," the Peregrine Volume One**]. Abigail Cross is born in Tennessee.

1910 – Evelyn Gould is born.

1912 – Byron Mendicott travels to France to kill Lucy Hale. [**The Chronicles of Lilith**]

1913 – Felix Cole meets the Cockroach Man and becomes part of The Great Work. [**"The Great Work," The Family Grace: An Extraordinary History**] Bart Hill is born in Sovereign City [Revealed in **The Adventures of Lazarus Gray Volume 14**]

1914 – Margaret Davies passes away in her sleep. Max is adopted by his uncle Reginald.

1915 – Felix Cole marries Charlotte Grace, Eobard Grace's cousin.

1916 – Leonid Kaslov's father Nikolai becomes involved in the plot to assassinate Rasputin.

1917 – Betsy Cole is born to Felix and Charlotte Grace Cole. Nikolai Kaslov is murdered.

1918 – Max Davies begins wandering the world. Richard Winthrop's parents die in an accident.

1922 – Warlike Manchu tutors Max Davies in Kyoto.

1925 – Max Davies becomes the Peregrine, operating throughout Europe.

1926 – Charlotte Grace dies. Richard Winthrop has a brief romance with exchange student Sarah Dumas.

1927 – Richard Winthrop graduates from Yale. On the night of his graduation, he is recruited into The Illuminati. Max and Leopold Grace battle the Red Lord in Paris. Richard Winthrop meets Miya Shimada in Japan, where he purchases The McGuinness Obelisk for The Illuminati. Bart Hill begins adventuring as a teenaged Daredevil.

1928 – The Peregrine returns to Boston. Dexter van Melkebeek [later to be known as The Darkling] receives his training in Tibet from Tenzin. Sheridan Masters loses his fiance Carmen in a terrible mystic storm in Egypt. He is trapped in Carcosa for several years.

1929 – Max Davies is one of the judges for the Miss Beantown contest **["The Miss Beantown Affair," The Peregrine Volume Three]**. Richard Winthrop destroys a coven of vampires in Mexico.

1930 – Richard Winthrop pursues The Devil's Heart in Peru **["Eidolon," Lazarus Gray Volume Three]**.

1932 – The Peregrine hunts down his father's killer **["Origins," the Peregrine Volume One]**. The Darkling returns to the United States.

1933 – Jacob Trench uncovers Lucifer's Cage. **["Lucifer's Cage", the Peregrine Volume One]** The Peregrine battles Doctor York **[All-Star Pulp Comics # 1]** After a failed attempt at betraying The Illuminati, Richard Winthrop wakes up on the shores of Sovereign City with no memory of his name or past. He has only one clue to his past in his possession: a small medallion adorned with the words Lazarus Gray and the image of a naked man with the head of a lion. **["The Girl With the Phantom Eyes," Lazarus Gray Volume One]**. The man who would eventually call himself Paul Alfred Müller-Murnau arrives in Sovereign on the same night as Lazarus Gray. **["Nemesis, "Lazarus Gray Volume Six]**.

1934 – Now calling himself Lazarus Gray, Richard Winthrop forms Assistance Unlimited in Sovereign City. He recruits Samantha Grace, Morgan Watts and Eun Jiwon **["The Girl With the Phantom Eyes," Lazarus Gray Volume One]** Walther Lunt aids German scientists in unleashing the power of Die Glocke, which in turn frees the demonic forces of Satan's Circus **["Die Glocke," Lazarus Gray Volume Two]**. The entity who will become known as The Black Terror is created **["The Making of a Hero," Lazarus Gray Volume Two]**.

1935 – Felix Cole and his daughter Betsy seek out the Book of Eibon. **["The Great Work," The Family Grace: An Extraordinary History]** Assistance Unlimited undertakes a number of missions, defeating the likes of Walther Lunt, Doc Pemberley, Malcolm Goodwill & Black Heart, Princess Femi & The Undying, Mr. Skull, The Axeman and The Yellow Claw **["The Girl With the Phantom Eyes," "The Devil's Bible," "The Corpse Screams at Midnight," "The Burning Skull," "The Axeman of Sovereign City,"** and **"The God of Hate," Lazarus Gray Volume One]** The Peregrine journeys to Sovereign City and teams up with Assistance Unlimited to battle Devil Face. They also encounter a new hero – The Dark Gentleman. **["Darkness, Spreading Its Wings of Black," The Peregrine Volume Two** and **Lazarus Gray Volume One]**. Lazarus Gray and Assistance Unlimited become embroiled in the search for Die Glocke **["Die Glocke," Lazarus Gray Volume Two]**

1936 – Assistance Unlimited completes their hunt for Die Glocke and confronts the threat of Jack-In-Irons. Abigail Cross and Jakob Sporrenberg join Assistance Unlimited **["Die Glocke," Lazarus Gray Volume Two]**. The Peregrine moves to Atlanta and recovers the Dagger of Elohim from Felix Darkholme. The Peregrine meets Evelyn Gould. The Peregrine battles Jacob Trench. **["Lucifer's Cage", the Peregrine Volume One]**. Reed Barrows revives Camilla. **["Kingdom of Blood," The Peregrine Volume One]**. Kevin Atwill is abandoned in the Amazonian jungle by his friends, a victim of the Gorgon legacy. **["The Gorgon Conspiracy," The Peregrine Volume One]**. Nathaniel Caine's lover is killed by Tweedledum while Dan Daring looks on **["Catalyst," The Peregrine Volume One]** Assistance Unlimited teams up with The Black Terror to battle Prometheus and The Titan in South America **["The Making of a Hero," Lazarus Gray Volume Two]**. Doc Pemberley allies himself with Abraham Klee, Stanley Davis and Constance Majestros to form Murder Unlimited. Lazarus Gray is able to defeat this confederation of evil and Pemberley finds himself the victim of Doctor Satan's machinations **["Murder Unlimited," Lazarus Gray Volume Three]**. Lazarus Gray is forced to compete with The Darkling for possession of a set of demonic bones. During the course of this, a member of Assistance Unlimited becomes Eidolon. **["Eidolon," Lazarus Gray Volume Three]**. Charity Grace dies and is reborn as the first female Gravedigger. **[Gravedigger Volume One]**. Dr. York attempts to revive Princess Femi so that she can aid him in battling The Peregrine **["The Peregrine Animated Script," The Peregrine Volume Three]**. The Dark Gentleman confronts The Shadow Court and brings them to justice. **["The Judgment of the Shadow Court," The Adventures of The Dark Gentleman Book One]**. A few weeks later, The Dark Gentleman learns the truth about Amadeus Crouch **["The Silver Room," The Adventures of The Dark Gentleman Book Two]**.

1937 – Max and Evelyn marry. Camilla attempts to create the Kingdom of Blood. World's ancient vampires awaken and the Peregrine is 'marked' by Nyarlathotep. Gerhard Klempt's experiments are halted. William McKenzie becomes Chief of Police in Atlanta. The Peregrine meets Benson, who clears his record with the police. **["Kingdom of Blood," the Peregrine Volume One]**. Lazarus Gray and Assistance Unlimited teams up with Thunder Jim Wade to confront the deadly threat of Leviathan **["Leviathan Rising", Lazarus Gray Volume Four]**. Hank Wilbon is murdered, leading to his eventual resurrection as the Reaper. **["Kaslov's Fire, "The Peregrine Volume One]**. The Peregrine and Evelyn become unwelcome guests of Baron Werner Prescott, eventually foiling his attempts to create an artificial island and a weather-controlling weapon for the Nazis **["The Killing Games, " The Peregrine Volume Three]** Gravedigger confronts a series of terrible threats in Sovereign City, including Thanatos, a gender-swapping satanic cult and The Headless Horseman. Charity and Samantha Grace make peace about their status as half-sisters. **[Gravedigger Volume One]** Lazarus Gray teams with Eidolon and The Darkling to combat Doctor Satan **["Satan's Circus," Lazarus Gray Volume Four]**. Lazarus Gray battles the forces of Wilson Brisk and Skyrider. The Three Sisters are unleashed upon Sovereign City **["The Felonious Financier," Lazarus Gray Volume Five]**. Gravedigger confronts the twin threats of Hiroshi Tamaki and the immortal known as Pandora **[Gravedigger Volume Two]**. Lazarus Gray travels to Cape Noire to investigate the mysterious vigilante known as Brother Bones **["Shadows and Phantoms, "Lazarus Gray Volume Five]**. The villain known as The Basilisk attempts to seize control of Sovereign City's underworld **["Stare of The Basilisk," Lazarus Gray Volume Five]**. The Three Sisters unite with Princess Femi to combat Assistance Unlimited. Sobek's attempt to destroy Femi helps lead young Madison Montgomery into a role as Femi's handmaiden. Lazarus gets engaged to Kelly Emerson **["Immortals," Lazarus Gray Volume**

Five]. Lazarus and Kelly are married. ["**Wedding Bells**," **Lazarus Gray Volume Five**]

1938 – The Peregrine travels to Great City to aid the Moon Man in battling Lycos and his Gasping Death. The Peregrine destroys the physical shell of Nyarlathotep and gains his trademark signet ring. ["**The Gasping Death**," **The Peregrine Volume One**]. The jungle hero known as the Revenant is killed ["**Death from the Jungle**," **The Peregrine Volume Two**]. Gravedigger, Lazarus Gray and The Peregrine come together to confront the terrible events known as Götterdämmerung. Many other heroes – including The Black Bat, The Black Terror, The Darkling and Leonid Kaslov are caught up in the events, as well. The insane villain Mr. Death is created. [**Götterdämmerung**]. Three months after Götterdämmerung, Assistance Unlimited battles The Librarian and adds The Black Terror to the team. ["The Affair of the Familiar Corpse," Lazarus Gray Volume Six]. Assistance Unlimited journeys to Europe where they reunite with Eidolon and Abby. The group then teams up with a Berlin-based hero known as Nakam to battle Mr. Death and The Torch. Lazarus Gray confronts the spirit of Walther Lunt and Baba Yaga. ["**The Strands of Fate**," **Lazarus Gray Volume Six**]. Mortimer Quinn is elected mayor of Sovereign City. Paul Alfred Müller-Murnau learns of his role as Nemesis and becomes an ally of Princess Femi and Madison Montgomery. Femi gains possession of the fabled Emerald Tablet. Abby becomes warden of Tartarus. ["**Nemesis,**" **Lazarus Gray Volume Six**]. Assistance Unlimited battles an out-of-control Golem and an agent of the OFP codenamed Heidi Von Sinn. Kelly's pregnancy takes an odd turn after exposure to an Aryan idol. ["**Tapestry**," **Lazarus Gray Volume Six**]. Daniel Higgins bonds with the Hell-forged armor and becomes Babylon. His sister Stella is killed. [**The Second Book of Babylon**]

1939 – Ibis and the Warlike Manchu revive the Abomination. Evelyn becomes pregnant and gives birth to their first child, a boy named William. ["**Abominations,**" **The Peregrine Volume One**]. The Peregrine allies himself with Leonid Kaslov to stop the Reaper's attacks and to foil the plans of Rasputin. ["**Kaslov's Fire**," **the Peregrine Volume One**] Violet Cambridge and Will McKenzie become embroiled in the hunt for a mystical item known as The Damned Thing [**The Damned Thing**] Assistance Unlimited teams up with Sheridan Masters to investigate a deadly alliance between Femi and a masked villain called El Demonio. The evils summon Hastur, the King In Yellow, and Lazarus is forced to travel to Carcosa. Kelly learns that their unborn child is infused with Vril energy. Femi and Madison Montgomery are both apparently destroyed. **[Lazarus Gray Volume Seven]**. Gravedigger engages in a war of wits with The King, a battle that leaves The Dark Gentleman dead and her forces in disarray. She uncovers the connection between The Voice and Nestorius – then stands for judgment before Anubis. **[Gravedigger Volume Three]**. Lazarus and Kelly Gray become the parents of Ezekiel Gray, Samantha Grace learns she's pregnant **["The Santa Slaying", Lazarus Gray Volume Eight]**.

1940 - Samantha discovers that Paul Alfred Müller-Murnau is responsible for her mystic pregnancy. Müller-Murnau forms a new version of Murder Unlimited alongside Bushido, Brick, Vixen and Alloy. **["As Above, So Below," Lazarus Gray Volume Eight]**. The Warlike Manchu returns with a new pupil — Hans Merkel, aka Shinigami. The Warlike Manchu kidnaps William Davies but the Peregrine and Leonid Kaslov manage to rescue the boy. **["Blitzkrieg, "the Peregrine Volume One]** The Peregrine journeys to Germany alongside the Domino Lady and Will McKenzie to combat the demonic organization known as Bloodwerks. **["Bloodwerks," the Peregrine Volume One]** Lazarus Gray encounters Gravedigger and a heroine from another universe while in Istanbul. The trio end up battling an alliance between Princess Femi and a villain from another world. A loosely-affiliated grouping of female heroes consisting of Lady Peregrine **[Evelyn Davies]**, Jet Girl, Fantomah and Kitten is formed. **[Worlds Apart]**. Samantha Grace gives birth to her daughter Emily. Assistance Unlimited battle a werewolf and free a young woman whose dreams are incredibly powerful **["The Girl That Dreamed, "Lazarus Gray Volume Eight]**. Kevin Atwill seeks revenge against his former friends, bringing him into conflict with the Peregrine **["The Gorgon Conspiracy," The Peregrine Volume One]**. The Peregrine takes a young vampire under his care, protecting him from a cult that worships a race of beings known as The Shambling Ones. With the aid of Leonid Kazlov, the cult is destroyed /"The Shambling Ones," The Peregrine Volume One]. Daniel Higgins and his sister Stella stumble onto a mob killing and Stella is badly injured. Daniel finds a strange suit of armor and bonds with it, becoming transformed into Babylon **[The Second Book of Babylon]**. Lazarus Gray and Assistance

Unlimited travel to Kentucky to investigate the disappearance of a young girl. Eidolon quits the team after a debate about how to resolve the crisis **["It Wants To Kill You," Lazarus Gray Volume Eight]**. Nemesis and Bushido join up with the Occult Forces Project to resurrect The Speaker from the Stars. They are opposed and ultimately foiled by Assistance Unlimited and The Golden Amazon **["The Speaker from the Stars," Lazarus Gray Volume Eight]**.

1941 – Philip Gallagher, a journalist, uncovers the Peregrine's secret identity but chooses to become an ally of the vigilante rather than reveal it to the world **["Origins," the Peregrine Volume One]**. The Peregrine teams with the Black Bat and Ascott Keane, as well as a reluctant Doctor Satan, in defeating the plans of the sorcerer Arias **["The Bleeding Hells", The Peregrine Volume One]**. The Peregrine rescues McKenzie from the Iron Maiden **["The Iron Maiden," The Peregrine Volume One]**. Asgard falls and Thor's hammer ends up in the hands of his daughter, whose spirit is hidden away in the body of a young woman on Earth. Loki and his assistant Durok end up working alongside Murder Unlimited [Nemesis, Bushido, The Golden Amazon and Eidolon] to try and flood the world so that it can remade along Loki's wishes. In the hidden world of Vorium, Assistance Unlimited teams with The Fighting Yank to foil their plans. The Golden Amazon and The Fighting Yank both become occasional members of Assistance Unlimited. Nemesis and Bushido are both killed. **["The Sinking World," Lazarus Gray Volume Nine]**. In November, The Golden Amazon, The Fighting Yank and The Black Terror journey to Manhattan to team with Olga Mesmer to stop a plot by Doctor Satan and his consort [Lady Satan]. The foursome remain together as The Heroes, an offshoot organization of Assistance Unlimited. The Black Terror agrees to serve as a liaison between the teams. **["Satan's Lair", Lazarus Gray Volume Ten]**. Tommy McDuff is injured during the attack on Pearl Harbor – he is taken from the military hospital by Eris, the Goddess of Discord. She gave him great power but at the cost of his sanity – as Phasma, he embarked on a scheme to use 'The Torch of Ç'thalpa to tear down many of the institutions of power. He worked with Rosemary Lunt [the daughter of Walther Lunt] and was opposed by Assistance Unlimited and Babylon. The villainous Billhook releases damaging information about Assistance Unlimited to the press. Lazarus Gray agrees to work with Major Caruso and Project: Cicada. **[Lazarus Gray Volume Ten]**.

1942 – The Peregrine battles a Nazi super agent known as the Grim Reaper, who is attempting to gather the Crystal Skulls **["The Three Skulls," The Peregrine Volume One]**. The Peregrine becomes embroiled in a plot by Sun Koh and a group of Axis killers known as The Furies. The Peregrine and Sun Koh end up in a deadly battle on the banks of the Potomac River. **["The Scorched God," The Peregrine Volume Two]**. In London, the Peregrine and Evelyn meet Nathaniel Caine [aka the Catalyst] and Rachel Winters, who are involved in stopping the Nazis from creating the Un Earth. They battle Doctor Satan and the Black Zeppelin **["Catalyst," The Peregrine Volume One]**. Evelyn learns she's pregnant with a second child. The Peregrine solves the mystery of the Roanoke Colony **["The Lost Colony," The Peregrine Volume One]**. The Peregrine battles against an arsonist in the employ of Bennecio Tommasso **["Where There's Smoke", The Peregrine Volume Three]**. The Warlike Manchu is revived and embarks upon a search for the Philosopher's Stone **["The Resurrection Gambit," The Peregrine Volume One]**. Joseph Williams is born [son of Mitchell and Charity]. Assistance Unlimited is forced to work with Nakam and Lilith [leader of the Crimson Ladies] to stop a plot formulated by a mystic named Woland and The Black Terror's archenemy, The Puzzler. The dead are raised in Sovereign City but Lazarus and his allies are able to eventually turn the tide with an assist from The Revenant and Baba Yaga. In the end, a shocking revelation is made that alters Morgan Watts' life forever. **[The Adventures of Lazarus Gray Volume Eleven]**.

1943 – The Peregrine teams with Xander to deal with the Onyx Raven **["The Onyx Raven", The Peregrine Volume Three]**. The Peregrine is confronted by the twin threats of Fernando Pasarin and the undead pirate Hendrik van der Decken **["The Phantom Vessel," The Peregrine Volume Two]**. Evelyn and Max become the parents of a second child, Emma Davies. The Peregrine teams with the daughter of the Revenant to battle Hermann Krupp and the Golden Goblin **["Death from the Jungle," The Peregrine Volume Two]** The Peregrine battles Doctor Satan over possession of an ancient Mayan tablet **["The Four Peregrines," The Peregrine Volume Two]**. The Peregrine travels to Peru to battle an undead magician called The Spook **["Spook," The Peregrine Volume Two]**. The Peregrine clashes with Doctor Death, who briefly takes possession of Will McKenzie **["The Peregrine**